"I'm going to say s~~~~~~~~~~~~~~~~~~ make us both a little uncomfortable.

"Which is surprising. I'm not usually so bold. But I feel like in our case we'd both rather have everything out in the open."

"Speak your mind," Trent prompted her.

Sydney drew another long breath and released it. "Is it my imagination or is something happening here? Between us, I mean."

His response was instant. "It's not your imagination."

She didn't know whether to be relieved or agitated. "The lieutenant warned me about you."

"What did he say?"

"That you're damaged goods."

His voice lowered to an intimate murmur. "He's not wrong. Maybe you should listen to him."

"You're not damaged. You're wounded. There's a difference."

"Is there?"

"Yes," she insisted.

Something flickered in his eyes. Doubt? Regret? Unease? She suddenly had second thoughts about her own honesty.

"Now I really have made you uncomfortable."

THE KILLER NEXT DOOR

AMANDA STEVENS

INTRIGUE

If you purchased this book without a cover you should be aware that this
book is stolen property. It was reported as "unsold and destroyed" to the
publisher, and neither the author nor the publisher has received any
payment for this "stripped book."

 **Harlequin®**
INTRIGUE™

Recycling programs
for this product may
not exist in your area.

ISBN-13: 978-1-335-45692-2

The Killer Next Door

Copyright © 2024 by Marilyn Medlock Amann

All rights reserved. No part of this book may be used or reproduced in any manner
whatsoever without written permission.

Without limiting the author's and publisher's exclusive rights, any unauthorized use of
this publication to train generative artificial intelligence (AI) technologies is expressly
prohibited.

This is a work of fiction. Names, characters, places and incidents are either the
product of the author's imagination or are used fictitiously. Any resemblance to
actual persons, living or dead, businesses, companies, events or locales is entirely
coincidental.

For questions and comments about the quality of this book, please contact us at
CustomerService@Harlequin.com.

TM and ® are trademarks of Harlequin Enterprises ULC.

 Harlequin Enterprises ULC
22 Adelaide St. West, 41st Floor
Toronto, Ontario M5H 4E3, Canada
www.Harlequin.com

Printed in Lithuania

MIX
Paper | Supporting
responsible forestry
FSC® C021394

Amanda Stevens is an award-winning author of over fifty novels, including the modern gothic series The Graveyard Queen. Her books have been described as eerie and atmospheric and "a new take on the classic ghost story." Born and raised in the rural South, she now resides in Houston, Texas, where she enjoys binge-watching, bike riding and the occasional margarita.

Books by Amanda Stevens

Harlequin Intrigue

Pine Lake
Whispering Springs
Digging Deeper
The Secret of Shutter Lake
The Killer Next Door

A Procedural Crime Story

Little Girl Gone
John Doe Cold Case
Looks That Kill

An Echo Lake Novel

Without a Trace
A Desperate Search
Someone Is Watching

Twilight's Children

Criminal Behavior
Incriminating Evidence
Killer Investigation

Visit the Author Profile page at Harlequin.com.

CAST OF CHARACTERS

Detective Sydney Shepherd—While on suspension from the police department, Sydney becomes convinced her next-door neighbor is a serial killer. Desperate to prevent the next murder, she agrees to work with a washed-up detective she helped get fired.

Trent Gannon—The disgraced police detective turned private investigator agrees to help Sydney with an off-the-books investigation. But can he put aside past grievances long enough to catch the Seaside Strangler?

Brandan Shaw—Is he a lone wolf or following in the footsteps of a mentor?

Lieutenant Dan Bertram—Sydney's superior is all too familiar with the unsolved serial murders that plagued the area two decades ago. He was in a position not only to cover his tracks, but also to groom his protégé.

Martin Swann—Twenty years ago, Sydney's landlord took a troubled adolescent under his wing, but to what end?

Richard Mathison—His youngest son stands accused of murdering his girlfriend. Is his other son—his forgotten son—a serial killer desperate for his father's attention?

Gabriel Mathison—Is he innocent of murder or the product of a dark legacy?

Chapter One

Suspended.

The dreaded word reverberated like a drumbeat inside Detective Sydney Shepherd's head, keeping time with the dull throb from her concussion. Her stomach churned as she mentally replayed the high-speed chase that had culminated in a single-vehicle car crash and a trip to the nearest ER in Seaside, Texas.

Even now she shuddered at the weightless sensation of being airborne and then the sickening crunch of metal against pavement as her vehicle rolled not once but twice before coming to a spinning stop that had left her battered, disoriented and upside down. A cacophony of honking horns and screeching brakes had finally propelled her into action. Untangling herself from the seat belt, she'd climbed through the shattered window to make sure no one else had been injured.

Later at the hospital, the ER doctor had been blunt. *You're lucky to be alive, young lady.*

Yeah, no kidding. Not that she needed his censure. She'd done nothing but berate herself since crawling through that broken window.

What were you thinking, pursuing a vehicle at that speed?

I was thinking I wanted to catch a killer before he fled

the country. I was thinking I wanted to wipe that smug smile from Gabriel Mathison's face once and for all. I was thinking of that moment when I could finally slap the cuffs on his wrists and read him his rights.

Liar. You weren't thinking at all. You let adrenaline and obsession take the wheel. You're damn lucky to be alive and even more fortunate that you didn't kill or maim someone else in the process.

Maybe death wouldn't have been such a bad option, she decided. Which was worse—living with the nagging torment of what could have happened or the sinking dread of what was about to happen?

Not to mention the fiery agony of a fractured ankle and the suffocating pressure from a bruised rib. It hurt to talk, it hurt to cough, it hurt to breathe. She lay flat on her back and stared at the ceiling in gloomy silence. *You deserve every bit of this misery. Thanks to you, Gabriel Mathison is now untouchable. He's probably out there at this very moment celebrating his victory.*

"Syd? Did you hear what I said?"

She dropped her gaze from the ceiling to the middle-aged man at the foot of the bed. Drawing a painful breath, she released it slowly. "Yes, I heard you. You said I'm suspended without pay, pending a full investigation."

"I said more than that." For a moment, Lieutenant Dan Bertram let his professional demeanor slip, and a fatherly concern flickered across his careworn features. "Are you in a lot of pain?"

She used every ounce of her strength not to groan. "Nothing I can't handle."

His tone turned gruff. "You don't have to do that, you know. Pretend you're unbreakable. This is me you're talking to. I used to patch up your skinned knees when you were little. You don't always have to be the toughest cop in the room."

Yes, I do. Not everyone is like you.

Even in this day and age, there were those in the department who would relish the chance to cut her down to size if they caught even a shred of vulnerability. The suit of armor she'd donned in the academy had eventually become a second skin, one never to be shed on duty or off. But she decided to throw the lieutenant a bone. "Okay, even my eyeballs hurt. Is that what you wanted to hear?"

"If it's the truth. When I got the call—" he paused as a myriad of emotions flashed across his features "—they sent me a photo of your car. I didn't know what to expect when I walked through that door."

"I'm sorry to worry you. The doctor says I'll be fine."

"Thank God for that." He seemed to wear the weight of the world on his slumping shoulders as he stood gazing down at her. His uniform was starting to tug across the middle and beneath his receding hairline, his brow had deepened into a perpetual scowl. He'd been divorced for nearly a decade, but he still sometimes fiddled with an imaginary wedding ring when he was worried or deep in thought. Before Sydney's dad had died, the two men had been partners and later close friends. Dan Bertram had been the nearest thing she'd had to a doting uncle long before he'd become her mentor and finally her commander. He expected a lot from her, and his obvious disappointment was a hard pill for Sydney to swallow.

"It could have been worse," she said.

"Much worse," he agreed. "You're young. You'll heal. And the suspension isn't permanent."

"We both know that's a mere formality. Even if by some miracle I'm allowed to stay on the force, I'll be busted down to patrol or desk duty. I'll never be allowed anywhere near the Criminal Investigations Unit again. Richard Mathison will see to that. He promised to rain hell down upon me if I went after his son. It wasn't an idle threat."

"Yet, you went after him anyway."

"I followed the evidence. You would have done the same."

The lieutenant sighed. "We're talking about you right now and the consequences of your actions. I'll ask the chief to have a word with Mathison. They're old friends. Maybe she can get him to call off the dogs. Avoiding a lawsuit will go a long way toward rehabilitating your reputation within the department."

Sydney wasn't buying it. "Why would the chief go out on a limb for me? Why would you, for that matter? You've got your own career to consider."

"Don't worry about me. I know how to protect myself. As to why... I made a promise years ago that I'd look out for you, and I don't go back on my word. Besides—" a rare smile tugged at his cheeks "—I see something of my younger self in you. I know what it's like to have a fire in your belly. That burning need to make a name for yourself. I know how dangerous it can be, too. Your dad cut me a break once when I was still green and ambitious, and I'm willing to do the same for you on one condition."

Her gaze narrowed. "What?"

"Use your recovery time to reflect on your choices. I'm dead serious about that. You need to reevaluate your priorities. Your dad set a high bar, and no one knows better than I the difficulty of living up to Tom Shepherd's standards." The lieutenant leaned in. "But here's the thing you need to remember. He wasn't born a hero. His legacy wasn't created overnight. He made mistakes along the way just like everyone else. You've been a detective for less than two years. You've still got a lot to learn. If Tom were here now, he'd be the first to tell you that patience and discretion are virtues. You have to know when to back off."

The advice didn't sit well with Sydney. She didn't like being manipulated, and she didn't believe for a moment that her dad would have let a guy like Gabriel Mathison walk because his family had clout and money. "You mean back off when the suspect has a wealthy father who also happens to be a member of the town council?"

The lieutenant's demeanor hardened in the face of her defiance. "It's called politics. Living to fight another day. You let your emotions get the better of you this time. You became so single-minded in your pursuit of Gabriel Mathison that you allowed him to goad you into making it personal."

Anger bubbled despite her best efforts. She took a calming breath and counted to ten. "Mathison thinks he's above the law. He thinks he can get away with murder because of who his father is. You and I both know he killed Jessica King. He attacked her with a blunt force instrument, strangled her while she lay unconscious and dumped her body on the side of the road. Then he partied with his friends for the rest of the night. If that isn't cold-blooded, I don't know what is."

"Knowing and proving are two different things. And, unfortunately, those same friends have given him an alibi for the time in question."

"Then we need to break them. We need to persuade one of them to come forward and tell the truth."

"You've tried that already."

"Obviously, I didn't try hard enough. That's on me." She paused to tamp down her emotions yet again. "I know you don't want to hear this, but what if I'm right? What if Jessica King wasn't his first victim? He has a violent history that his father has worked very hard to conceal. What if Gabriel Mathison was the perpetrator of at least two other unsolved homicides in the past year?"

Her steely resolve deepened his scowl. "You're right. I don't want to hear it. That's the kind of overreach that got you into trouble in the first place."

"I know that."

"Do you? Because your actions suggest otherwise." She tried to protest, but he put up a hand to halt her. "Just listen for once. I stuck my neck out for you. You were allowed to take lead on the Jessica King case at my request. Your first homicide investigation should have been a big opportunity for you, but you went too far. You couldn't nail Mathison on the case you were assigned, so you started digging for connections that were at best weak and at worst far-fetched. You acted impulsively, some might say irrationally, and now here we are."

His frank assessment of her performance was like a dagger through her heart. Turning her head to the narrow window, she fixed her gaze on the parking lot while blinking back hot tears. "Do you really think it's a coincidence that the victim's best friend was transferred to another state after claiming Jessica was afraid of Gabriel? Or that the witness who saw a physical altercation between Gabriel and Jessica the night she was murdered suddenly decided to recant her story? Richard Mathison is cleaning up his son's mess just like he's always done. Why would he go to all that trouble if Gabriel is innocent? Three victims in the past year, all strangled, their bodies found along the interstate just miles from the Mathison beach house. I suppose that's also a coincidence."

"Think about what you just said. Why would he dispose of bodies so close to his family's property?"

She turned back to him. "Why not, if he thinks he's untouchable?"

"Okay." The lieutenant's voice became deceptively calm, but any hint of patience or support had long since vanished. "Let's go through this one more time. The first victim was found in the trunk of an abandoned car, the second a few months later in a shallow grave. Both had been bound and strangled, both had close ties to the drug trade. That's a dangerous lifestyle. Executions are as common as handshakes. Jessica King was an associate at a respected law firm. She came from a good family with no known ties to the cartels or any other criminal enterprise. Despite your efforts to the contrary, you haven't been able to link her murder to the other two homicides."

"Except for how she was murdered. Two strangulations might be a coincidence, but three is a pattern," Sydney insisted.

"You're doing it again. You just can't help yourself, can you?"

Her chin came up. "All I know is that sweeping inconvenient facts under the rug won't make them go away. Something very real and very dark is happening in our little community. A killer is out there preying on young women. I don't know how or why, but every instinct is telling me that Gabriel Mathison is somehow involved."

"That kind of talk doesn't leave this room, Detective." The formality of his admonishment underscored his warning. He was no longer a caring friend or even a concerned mentor, but a commanding officer putting her on notice. "The last thing we want is to scare people into thinking we have an active serial killer in the area.

"As for Mathison—" he straightened and returned to the foot of her bed "—he's no longer your concern. Under no circumstances will you make contact with him. If you pass him on the street, look the other way. From this moment forward, that man is dead to you. Am I clear?"

She swallowed a retort and nodded.

"Keep your mouth shut and your head down until this situation is resolved one way or another. In the meantime, I would advise that you give some thought to what you'll say if and when you go before the review board. Don't get defensive and don't be afraid to show remorse. A little humility can go a long way."

Defiance crept into her reply despite her best efforts. "Even when I know I'm right?"

His icy glare spoke volumes. "Learn to play the game, or get used to writing parking tickets."

SYDNEY CONTEMPLATED THE lieutenant's warning while she waited for the doctor to return. Depending on the results of the CT scan, she could be released as soon as her broken bone was set. That was her hope, at least. A night in the hospital was the last thing she wanted. The teeming misery of the emergency room made her long for the quiet sanctuary of her tiny garage apartment.

She also needed access to her laptop. As luck would have it, she'd downloaded her case notes to the hard drive, enabling her to continue a virtual investigation while she recuperated at home. The powers that be could remove her physically from the case and muzzle her contacts within the department, but they had no control over what she did on her own time in the privacy of her own home.

You're doing it again, Syd. The lieutenant's admonishment lingered like a bitter aftertaste. *You just can't help yourself, can you?*

Okay, so maybe he was right. A little reflection might be warranted after such a monumental screwup. Maybe she had allowed herself to become obsessed and single-minded. Maybe she did need to take a step back and regroup. But soul-searching had never been her strong suit. An honest evaluation required owning up to several unpleasant peccadillos, including a tendency toward hubris.

It didn't matter that her pride and arrogance came from a place of self-doubt. Deep down, she was daunted by the expectation of living up to her father's legacy and bedeviled by the fear that she would never escape his shadow. Her particular combination of fervency and aloofness was offputting. She had no real friends, no close relationships. Even her own mother kept her distance. But that particular rabbit hole was an exploration for another day.

A nurse came in a little while later to recheck her vitals and to inform her that she was being moved to a private room. When Sydney expressed dismay, he gave her a sympathetic smile. "Don't worry. You'll be out of here before you know it. For now, though, we'd like to keep an eye on you overnight. As soon as the order comes through, someone will be in to take you upstairs. But that may be a while, so just sit tight, okay? We don't want to lose you in all the confusion."

Sydney couldn't tell if he was joking or not.

While she waited alone in the tiny room, she practiced visualizing the pain leaving her body in a wisp of gray-green smoke. Guided imagery sometimes helped with the tension headaches she brought home from work. Normally, she tried to avoid strong painkillers, but right now she'd give her last paycheck for a shot of something to knock her out.

Forcing herself to concentrate on the imagery of that coil of smoke, she lay back against the pillow and closed her eyes. Surprisingly, she managed to drift off. She had the strangest dream about being wheeled into a section of the hospital under construction and left to fend for herself. When she tried to get up from the gurney, she discovered her wrists and ankles were shackled to the metal bed rails. She couldn't move or call for help. All she could do was watch in horror as a masked surgeon, whose eyes looked an awful lot like Gabriel Mathison's, materialized at her side with arms outstretched toward her neck.

She awoke on a gasp, her hand to her throat.

"You okay?" a voice asked from the doorway.

She turned her head toward the sound. A man stood just inside the room reading a file he'd plucked from the plastic holder on the door. He also wore a mask, but his head was bowed to the chart, so she couldn't see his eyes.

Her pulse accelerated as she watched him. He wasn't the doctor who had examined her earlier, and he didn't appear to be a nurse or attendant. He didn't look as if he belonged in the hospital at all, dressed as he was in faded jeans, sneakers and a plaid shirt that he wore open over a gray T-shirt. It came to her in a flash that he might be someone the Mathisons had sent to finish her off. She wanted to laugh at her imagination, but knowing what she knew about that family, the notion didn't seem that absurd.

She tried to project authority into her voice. "Who are you?"

He didn't glance up. "I just came by to see how you're doing."

"Are you a doctor?" Something about his voice, about

the way he kept his head lowered just enough so that she couldn't get a good look at him... "Where's Dr. Parnell?"

"I'm sure he'll be along soon." He dropped the file back in the holder and turned. "How's the pain?"

"Manageable." She gripped the edge of the bed, realizing how completely at this stranger's mercy she was. She couldn't run, much less fight, though she wouldn't go down without trying. "Who are you again?"

He strode into the room as if he had every right in the world to be there. When he got to the foot of the bed, he removed the paper mask and stuffed it in his shirt pocket.

She gaped at him in astonishment. *"Trent Gannon?"*

His gaze raked her from head to toe. "You remember my name. I'd say that's a good sign considering the head injury."

She swallowed back her shock. "Not necessarily. Some people are hard to forget under any circumstances."

"Thank you."

"It wasn't a compliment." She forced her gaze to remain steady when she really wanted to glance away from the boldness of his gray eyes. Of all the disgraced former police detectives to come strolling into her room. "How did you get back here anyway? They have restrictions on who can come and go from this area."

He shrugged. "I've always found that if you act like you belong, most people are reluctant to question you."

"Someone should speak to security about that," she muttered. *Trent Gannon.* She shook her head in disbelief. How long had it been anyway? She'd lost track of him years ago. "You still haven't told me why you're here."

"I was visiting a friend in the hospital. He had the TV on, and I heard your name mentioned in conjunction with a high-speed chase that ended in a crash. The local news showed a picture of the car." He gave a low whistle. "That's one less vehicle in the city fleet."

"So you came by to gloat?"

He lifted a brow at her curt tone. "Do you really think I'd take pleasure in someone else's misfortune?"

"Yes, I do. Don't you remember what you said to me the last time we met face-to-face?"

"That wasn't one of my better days." He moved back so that he could lean a shoulder against the wall. Disgraced or not, his presence filled that tiny room, so much so that Sydney found it a little difficult to catch her breath. She resisted the urge to pull the sheet up to her chin even though she was still fully clothed. "I'd just surrendered my shield and firearm and packed up my desk. I said a lot of things to a lot of people on my way out. But that was a long time ago. Water under the bridge as they say. I don't hold a grudge."

Sydney bristled. "I should hope not, considering everything that happened was your fault. You had to know you were risking your career when you decided to show up drunk to a crime scene."

Something that might have been regret flickered in his eyes. "When someone starts drinking on the job, they usually aren't thinking too clearly, period."

"I guess not." She hesitated, then said in a softer tone, "For the record, no one enjoyed watching your downfall."

His smile turned wry. "I don't know if that's entirely true."

"It is. A lot of people covered for you for as long as they could. Longer than they should have."

His smile disappeared. "But not you."

She met his gaze without flinching. "I had no choice. I was asked point-blank by my commanding officer what I witnessed at that crime scene. I had to tell the truth. You were becoming a danger to yourself and others."

"You did the right thing."

His response took her aback. He wasn't at all the way she remembered him. He'd once been considered the best detective in the Criminal Investigations Unit, someone who commanded respect and admiration from his peers and superiors alike. But at the height of his career, he'd already displayed a tendency to self-destruct. Considering the gossip and her memory of his ignominious departure, she would have expected an attack on her character or, at the very least, pushback on her recall of events. Instead, his easy acceptance of her criticism left her momentarily speechless.

In the ensuing silence, she tried to study his demeanor without being obvious. She'd once found Trent Gannon attractive, but that was back when he was still a hotshot detective with an unparalleled record for closing cases. His downward spiral had changed her perception of him, and in time he'd become a cautionary tale. Now she found herself unsettled by the similarities to her current trajectory.

"As you said, it was a long time ago," she murmured, for lack of anything better to offer.

"Three years can seem like a lifetime. I was headed down a bad path. It took me a long time to admit that you actually did me a favor. Losing my job made me take a cold, hard look at myself. I knew I needed to make changes. First, I had to stop drinking. I woke up one morning and decided to quit cold turkey."

"That couldn't have been easy."

"It wasn't, but probably not as hard as you imagine. I don't say that to diminish the hell others go through to get and stay sober. For me, booze was always more of a crutch than a craving. A liquid bandage. I didn't miss it after I quit. I sure as hell didn't miss the hangovers."

Why had she never wondered before what had driven him to drink? Why had she never been curious enough to ask? Too caught up in her own ambition, she supposed. She felt ashamed now to admit that her initial thought upon his departure from the department was that a spot in the Criminal Investigations Unit had finally opened up.

"I'm glad you're doing well," she said and meant it, though she wasn't sure if she believed him. Had he really changed his ways? His careless appearance would suggest otherwise. "It's admirable that you turned your life around, but I still don't understand what any of this has to do with me. We haven't spoken since you left. We were barely acquaintances even back then. Now here you are acting as if we're long-lost friends. I'd like to know why."

The inscrutable look he gave her sent a shiver of alarm down her spine. "It's simple. You helped me once. I'd like to return the favor."

"How?"

He came around to the side of the bed and pulled up a stool. "May I?" He sat without waiting for her consent. His nearness made her even more uneasy, but she didn't want to call attention to her distress by asking him to leave. If he was here to make amends, she didn't want to be the one to set him back.

She scanned his features, noting the fine lines around his eyes and mouth, the hairstyle that had grown a little too shaggy and the clothing that had seen better days. She wondered suddenly what his life had been like since he left the department. No one ever talked about him. It was as if Trent Gannon had vanished into thin air when he walked out the door that day.

"I've been following your case," he said. "For what it's worth coming from me, I think you're right about Gabriel

Mathison. Something is off about that guy. There've been rumors about him for years and how he likes to play rough with women. I don't know if he killed his girlfriend, but he's hiding something."

He had her full attention now. "What do you mean? Give me specifics."

He quelled her excitement. "I can't. It's instinct more than anything else. A gut feeling after watching his body language at his father's press conference. I'm still pretty good at reading people."

"Richard Mathison gave a press conference? That was fast. And…not good," she fretted. "For me, at least."

Trent nodded. "They played it off as improvised, but everyone knows he has the local media in his pocket. Not just the media. Plenty of important people in this town owe him favors. Some of them work for the police department. I've seen firsthand how evidence can disappear and witnesses will clam up after a single phone call from his office. But the kind of money that can be used to bribe and coerce can also make people arrogant and careless. Gabriel Mathison doesn't have his father's discipline. He's not capable of committing the perfect murder. If he's guilty, sooner or later, he'll let something slip. He'll talk to the wrong person. His ego won't allow him to remain silent."

She said on a resigned sigh, "I hope you're right, but I won't be the one to bring him in. I've been removed from the investigation and suspended without pay. If I go near Gabriel Mathison, I face termination and possibly a lawsuit." She cast a worried glance toward the hallway door. "I shouldn't even be talking to you about the case."

He lowered his voice. "I understand. They've put you on a short leash. Forget the nuts and bolts of the investigation. Tell me about the accident."

"Why?"

"I'd just like to hear from you what happened."

Sydney still didn't trust his motives. What if this amiable side of Trent Gannon was an act to disguise his vendetta? What if he was here to take advantage of her current vulnerability to somehow hasten her downfall? Anything was possible, but for the time being, she decided to give him the benefit of the doubt if for no other reason than the conversation distracted her from the searing pain in her ankle.

"I received an anonymous call that a plane was fueled and waiting on a private airstrip to fly Mathison across the border," she said. "Long story short, I staked out his place and then followed him onto the interstate when he left his house. He accelerated. I accelerated. Next thing I knew, a third vehicle came out of nowhere and cut me off. I swerved, hit the shoulder and rolled."

"Do you think you were set up?"

"I've wondered about that. But how could he have been so certain I'd take the bait, let alone that I'd lose control of my vehicle?"

"He knew you wouldn't take a chance on letting him leave the country. The third car was either meant to take you out or make the pursuit appear more dangerous and reckless than it was. Even without the crash, a high-speed chase would have been enough to trigger an investigation into your conduct. You likely would have been removed from the case regardless."

Sydney grimaced. "He outmaneuvered me. The lieutenant was right. I let my emotions get the better of me, and now I'm stuck in here while he's out there free to do as he pleases."

"That's why I'm here," Trent said. "If you're willing to take a chance on me, I can help you nail him. I can be your eyes and ears and even your driver until you're up and around and able to navigate on your own."

His offer stunned her. She searched for a telltale crack or twitch in his features as she wondered yet again why he'd turned up out of the blue the way he had. It couldn't be as simple as making amends. "As intriguing as I find the offer, you'll understand why I'm a little concerned about your motive."

"I just want to help."

Did he? "Even if I wanted or needed your help, I'm not allowed to go anywhere near Gabriel Mathison. If I so much as glance at him sideways, my suspension becomes permanent."

"True, but I'm a private citizen. I can do whatever I want within the law. Besides—" he leaned forward, his eyes still shadowed with something she couldn't read "—we both know you are never going to let this go, regardless of the consequences."

"You don't know anything about me."

A faint smile flickered. "I know a driven person when I see one. I'm offering you a way around your suspension. I do all the legwork and conduct the interviews. Your hands stay clean."

She frowned. "What do you want in return?"

He got up and moved back to the foot of the bed, as if what he had to say required a little distance. "For the past couple of weeks, I've been doing a deep dive into a series of murders that occurred in Southeast Texas from the late 1990s through the early 2000s. Roughly a quarter of a century ago. The bodies of seven young women were found in as many years along the I-45 corridor from Houston to Galveston. Are you familiar with those cases?"

"No, but I would have been a little kid back then. I was in kindergarten during the whole Y2K thing."

He nodded. "I was a few years older, but I didn't remember them, either, until I recently interviewed a retired Houston police detective on my podcast. He said—"

She cut him off. "Hold on. Your *podcast*?"

He looked amused. "Not what you expected from a former drunk?"

Hardly. Never in a million years would she have associated Trent Gannon with anything remotely connected to a podcast or social media in general. If someone had told her that he'd been found dead in a ditch somewhere or that he was serving time in a state penitentiary, yeah. Either of those scenarios would have been more believable.

His smile turned deprecating. "I'll admit, it's not the career I would have chosen for myself, but desperate times called for desperate measures. I started the podcast as a side hustle after I was fired. A way to make a few bucks while drumming up business for my private detective agency—"

She cut him off a second time. "You're a private detective now? Since when?"

"Since I needed to eat and pay bills and no one would hire me," he said with brutal honesty. "I was more surprised than anyone when the podcast took off, but that's a story for another day."

She took a moment to digest his revelations and to adjust her perception of him. Not dead in a ditch or serving time, but a man who'd pulled himself up from a very dark place and carved out a new career for himself. Would she have the courage to do the same?

He gave her a knowing look as if he could tell what she was thinking. "Should I go on?"

She nodded.

"The MO on those cases was all over the place. Shootings, stabbings, strangulations—"

"Strangulations?" Sydney bolted upright despite the bruised rib. Then she clutched her side and eased back down. "Sorry. Please continue."

"Different causes of death and bodies found in different locations. No apparent similarities or connections among the victims. No physical resemblances other than an age range. Nothing in common except for the fact that their murders went unsolved. By every indication, the homicides were random. Each case was investigated individually by the appropriate jurisdiction. Despite the disparities, a detective assigned to one of the cases began to suspect a single killer was responsible and requested assistance from the FBI. The information gathered from the various law enforcement agencies was consolidated and a common thread eventually identified. Articles of clothing and jewelry had been taken from each of the victims. Initially, it was assumed the items had been lost during captivity or a struggle. An earring, a scarf, a handbag. In every single case, at least one shoe was missing. Always the left shoe."

Sydney rubbed a hand up and down her arm where chill bumps had suddenly surfaced. "Why the left shoe?"

"Possibly some kind of fetish or disorder. Or a misdirection to fool the police." He shrugged. "One victim a year for seven years, and then the murders stopped. For whatever reason, the killer went dormant and the trail went cold. Very few people in the area ever realized that a serial predator had lived among them. May still live among us."

Sydney stared at him for the longest moment, almost afraid to say aloud the conclusion she'd immediately jumped to. "Are you suggesting he's active again?"

He seemed hesitant to answer. "It's a longshot. Odds are the killer is dead or in prison for another crime. But my gut tells me that maybe, just maybe, he's still out there. I'm trying to find another piece of the puzzle, no matter how small or seemingly insignificant. You may be able to help me."

"How?"

"Your dad was the local cop who brought in the FBI."

"What?" She pushed herself up against the pillows. "Are you sure?"

"Yes. You didn't know?"

She tried to conceal her shock. The conversation had taken a turn she hadn't expected. "He wouldn't have mentioned anything about it at home. My mother didn't like hearing about his cases."

"That's usually for the best." Something in his tone made her wonder again about his private life. "The fifth body was found in a wooded area off the freeway, but within the Seaside city limits. Your dad took lead. He'd been working the case for over a year when another body turned up in a remote area of Galveston County. This time, there were enough similarities to his case that he started to look into past unsolved homicides in the region. He began to suspect they were looking for a single perpetrator clever enough to disguise his movements and proclivities by varying his MO, victim selection and location. Rather than trying to coerce cooperation from the various jurisdictions, he decided to request assistance from the feds."

Sydney sat riveted. "What was the cause of death in his case?"

"Victim number five was the first of three strangulations."

"*Three* strangulations?" She tried to fight off a growing unease as something clicked into place. Maybe she did have a vague recollection of those cases. An overheard conversation between her parents niggled at the back of her mind.

Don't let her play outside alone until we catch the bastard.

She's a handful, Tom. I can't watch her twenty-four hours a day.

Trent pounced on her silence. "What's wrong? Did you remember something?"

"Not really. Nothing helpful." But the memory kept tugging. *She's a handful, Tom. I can't watch her twenty-four hours a day.* Even with the threat of a serial killer on the loose?

"Are you sure?" he pressed.

She sighed. "Like I said, I was just a little kid back then. As for my dad, he died a few years ago. And there's no way I can get my hands on his casefiles, if that's where you're going with this."

"You still have friends in the department, don't you?"

"No one who'll stick their neck out for me."

Except for Dan Bertram, although she'd done a pretty good job of burning that bridge earlier. Still, he'd been her dad's partner for years. The two had been like brothers for a time. Even if he hadn't been actively involved in the investigation, he would have known about the cases. Why hadn't he mentioned them in conjunction to the recent strangulations?

Trent said something, drawing her attention back to their conversation. "I'm sorry. What?"

"I asked about your dad's notebooks. Did he keep any records at home?"

"His personal belongings were put in storage when I sold the house. It would take hours to go through all the boxes."

"I'm willing if you are."

She gave him a long, penetrating stare. "Why didn't you tell me the truth from the start instead of trying to play me?"

"What do you mean?"

Her gaze narrowed. "Admit it. You don't give a damn about helping me. You just want access to my dad's files."

"Why can't it be both?"

At least he didn't insult her with a flat-out denial. "Why are you so interested in these cases anyway? What's in it for you? Are you trying to prove something? Or is it just about content for your podcast?"

"You didn't mention justice."

She folded her arms.

"Okay, you're right. It was about content in the beginning," he admitted. "The interview with the former HPD detective was one of my most popular shows. Thousands of new subscribers in a matter of days after I uploaded the video. Some of the clips from the episode went viral and racked up so many views that I decided to turn it into a series. People love police procedurals and unsolved mysteries. Podcasts are the new medium for true crime fanatics. But the deeper I dug…" He hesitated as if unsure how much he wanted to reveal. "Let's just say, I now have a more compelling reason for exploring these murders."

"What reason?"

"That's something I'm not yet ready to discuss."

"Being cryptic won't help your cause," she warned. "And anyway, I don't know that I'm comfortable letting you dig through my dad's things. He was a very private person."

"Will you at least think about it?"

She gave a vague nod. "I need to rest now."

"Yeah, I can see that. This isn't the time or place anyway. I'll be in touch. In the meantime, take care of yourself. I don't just mean physically." He came back around to the side of her bed and stared down at her. "Don't make the mistake of thinking the department will have your back. The moment

Richard Mathison files a lawsuit, they'll circle the wagons. You have no idea how bad it can get."

"I'm starting to have an inkling," she murmured.

He removed a card from his shirt pocket and placed it on top of the sheet. "If you find yourself out in the cold, give me a call."

Chapter Two

Late that afternoon, Sydney was moved upstairs to a private room with a nice view of downtown. The doctor had gone over the X-rays and CT scans, and then her temporary ankle splint was replaced with a fiberglass cast. If all went well for the next four to six weeks, she would then be fitted with a walking boot.

The cast was lightweight, but already her skin felt hot and itchy inside and elevating her foot soon became unbearable. She was tired of lying on her back, tired of being poked and prodded, just plain tired, period. But she reminded herself that a fractured ankle was nothing in the scheme of things. She'd made it through her father's death and had finally come to terms with her mother's indifference. A broken bone wasn't going to keep her down for long.

However, by the time the dinner hour rolled around, her spirits had flatlined, and she found herself nearly comatose with pain. Her tray came and went untouched. She tried to practice visualization as she waited for the pain meds to take effect. Checking emails and returning text messages only distracted her for a little while. Finally, she switched on the TV and dozed to the background drone of a garden show.

Drifting in and out, she noted the deepening shadows

outside her window as the nursing shift changed and a new face came in to check on her. When she finally fell into a deep sleep, she awakened abruptly, alarmed and disoriented as one often was in a strange place. She lay very still as her eyes adjusted to the darkness. A dull throb at her temples and the rigidity of the cast around her ankle brought everything back. The car crash, the suspension, the unexpected visit from Trent Gannon. She knew where she was and how she'd gotten there, but something seemed…not right.

She remained motionless as she tried to attune her senses to her surroundings. She heard the faint peal of a ringtone as someone moved down the hallway outside her door and the more distant ping of the elevator. She could smell roses. Someone must have brought in a bouquet while she slept. That was surprising. For a moment she wondered—hoped—the arrangement might be from her mother, but when had Lori Shepherd ever thought of anyone but herself? That was unfair. She probably didn't even know about the accident unless Dan Bertram had thought to call her.

Shaking off the remnants of sleep, Sydney started to reach for the light switch, then froze as she realized what had awakened her. Why goose bumps prickled at her nape. Someone was in her room.

She stifled a gasp as a silhouette took shape in the weak illumination from the bathroom nightlight. A man stood at the foot of her bed gazing down at her.

Her first instinct was to reach for her weapon until she remembered she'd surrendered her firearm to the lieutenant. She remained motionless in the dark, wanting desperately to believe that a nurse had come to check on her, but she knew better.

How long had he been standing there?

She ran through the possibilities as she lay perfectly still on the outside, but bracing herself on the inside.

It couldn't be Trent Gannon. He'd left hours ago, and he had no reason to return unless she called him. And the lieutenant or any of her colleagues wouldn't visit her room at such a late hour. Most of them would probably want to steer clear of her anyway for fear of being tainted by her suspension. The wagons had undoubtedly started to circle, leaving her out in the cold as Trent had predicted.

Gabriel Mathison. The name came with an icy certainty that set her heart to pounding. Adrenaline pulsed through her veins, tingling at her fingertips and the base of her spine. Still, she remained frozen, though a muscle in her wounded foot had started to twitch uncontrollably.

"I know you're awake." His voice sounded silky smooth in the shadowy room, edged with the kind of ingrained superiority that excess too often bred. Beneath the scent of the roses, she caught a hint of his cologne, something woodsy and expensive and suppressive. Something that reminded her of death.

"I can see you in the moonlight," he said. "Your eyes are wide open and gleaming. Are you frightened?"

In response, she slid her hand across the sheet, groping for the call button.

"It's not there," he informed her. "I put the controls and your phone out of reach. I thought it best we not be interrupted."

She swallowed back her fear. "I could scream. The nurse's station is just down the hall."

"You could, but you won't." He sounded supremely confident. "Your curiosity won't let you. Or maybe *obsession* is a better word."

Prove him wrong. Scream for help at the top your lungs.

Instead, she hoisted herself up against the pillows so that she didn't feel quite so vulnerable. "I'm not obsessed," she said. "I'm determined."

"And look where that got you." He leaned against the rail, tracing his finger down the side of her cast.

"Don't touch me." She jerked her foot away, sending a spasm of pain up her leg.

He gave a low laugh. "Don't worry. You're not my type. I've never cared for dirty blondes. But it seems you do have an admirer."

Her vision had adjusted to the darkness so that she could see him more clearly now, the dark hair falling just so across his forehead, the perfectly symmetrical features, the taunting smile. He might have been considered extraordinarily handsome if not for a weak jawline and the glint of cruelty in his eyes.

She needed to moisten her dry lips but she didn't want to give him the satisfaction of knowing how badly he unnerved her. Was she frightened? Yes. If her suspicions were true, he'd killed at least once and gotten away with it. Why wouldn't he think he could do so again?

"What admirer?" she found herself asking.

He gave a nod to the table beside her bed. "The white roses on your nightstand. At least two dozen, I would guess. Too extravagant to be from a friend or colleague. Someone obviously wants to make an impression." She could sense his smirk. "Shall I read the card to you?"

"Just tell me why you're here."

"See you soon, Sydney."

"What?"

"No signature on the card. Just…*See you soon, Sydney.*"

She swallowed back a wave of panic. "How do you know what the card says?"

"I took a peek while you were sleeping."

He'd been in her room long enough to read the message that came with the roses. To remove the call button and take her phone. He'd been that close while she lay sleeping. What else had he done?

Moving around to the side of the bed, he placed his body between her and the hallway door. He wasn't a big man. Two or three inches shy of six feet with a slim build. But she knew from her research that he was a kickboxer. He also held black belts in karate and aikido, and like his father, he had a fascination for antique weapons.

All of this ran through her mind while she sized up her chances of making a run for the door with a broken ankle.

He peered down at her. "You don't look so good."

She forced steel into her tone. "At least I'm alive. That's more than I can say for Jessica King."

He seemed unfazed by the mention of his dead girlfriend. "Yes, poor Jessie. So tragic. She was very nearly the perfect woman except for one tiny flaw." He leaned in so close that he could have easily slid his fingers around Sydney's throat or stuffed a pillow over her face. "Like you, she had the bad habit of sticking her nose where it didn't belong."

"Is that why you killed her?"

"See what I mean? Always asking questions."

"What happened?" Sydney struggled to keep her emotions static. Mathison was all about being in control. *Let him believe he has the upper hand. He might let something slip.* "Did she find out something about your father's business? About you? Did you kill her to keep her quiet?"

"You seem to think you have all the answers. You tell me." His voice was deceptively passive.

She gave a curt nod. "I think you attacked her in a fit of jealous rage. She was a beautiful, successful woman with any number of admirers. You didn't like her getting all that attention, so you decided to teach her a lesson. Rough her up a little. Show her who was really in control. But she fought you, didn't she? That's why you had to hit her. So hard you fractured her skull. Then you strangled her as she lay unconscious. You couldn't take a chance that she might survive. That she might wake up and tell someone what you'd done to her. Am I close? Come on," she coaxed. "Tell me what really happened. There's no one here but us. It'll be your word against mine."

"And who would ever believe you over me?" His eyes glittered dangerously as he stared down at her.

"Exactly," she agreed, even though the truth irked her. "You've already bested me. I've been removed from the case. Suspended without pay indefinitely. My credibility is shot and my career is over. No matter what you say, I can't touch you. So tell me what I missed. Tell me where I went wrong." She tried to keep her tone even as her fingers curled into fists beneath the covers. "That's why you're here, isn't it? To rub your win in my face."

"I'm here to make sure you got the message. But you're right about one thing. Your career is over. You tried to tarnish the Mathison name, and my old man won't stand for that. You have no idea how far he'll go to protect his precious reputation. This…" He waved a hand toward her cast. "Trust me, what happened to you in that crash is nothing compared to what's coming."

"I'm not afraid of your father. I'm not afraid of you, either," she lied. "You think you've gotten away with murder, but someone like you doesn't commit the perfect crime. Your ego makes you careless. You'll have overlooked some small detail, or maybe one of your friends will decide to rat you out. Badge or no badge, I'll be watching. I'll be waiting."

He gave an exaggerated shudder. "You're making me shiver."

"Sneer all you want," she said. "But this isn't over."

"You're right about that, too." He leaned down suddenly, placing his lips against her ear. "See you soon, Sydney."

TRENT GLANCED AT his phone on the table beside his worn-out beach chair. The metal frame creaked as he leaned sideways, and for the umpteenth time, he wondered when the thing would collapse altogether. He'd found it discarded behind the garage when he moved in last year, so he figured he and the chair had been living on borrowed time ever since.

He checked the clock on the screen as he'd done repeatedly for the past half hour. Nearly midnight. Finally. He'd been up since five that morning, going strong all day, and now he longed for the comfort of his bed. Instead, he stretched out his legs and waited.

The June night was unseasonably hot and sticky. Lightning flickered in the distance. He could smell ozone on the warm breeze that blew in from the water. Rain would be nice. The bedraggled tomato plant at the corner of his backyard could use a long drink. Maybe a storm would cool things off. Wishful thinking. Summer on the Gulf Coast could be brutal weatherwise. Droughts, flash flooding, the occasional hurricane to worry about. Not to mention mosquitos.

He thought about walking down to the dock and dangling his feet in the water while he waited. His neighbors, mostly retirees and ex-military, had long since turned in, so he didn't have to worry about making idle chitchat. Didn't have to pretend to care about fishing or cards or any of the mundane activities that filled their long days. He liked living alone for a reason. He briefly flirted with the idea of a quick dip, but instead he settled deeper into the chair. He was comfortable right where he was, so why bother? Besides, the view from his yard was hard to beat. Most people desired oceanfront property, but he preferred the bay. The water was calmer, his surroundings quieter. Sometimes a little too quiet, but he was used to the solitude.

Before the heat had set in, he sometimes slept on the screened porch, lulled by the breeze and the sound of lapping water as he drifted in and out of his dreams. For the last few nights, however, he'd taken to sleeping inside even when the weather was mild. He'd gotten into the habit of making an extra round through the house just to check the locks before he allowed his head to hit the pillow. On restless nights, he'd stand at the sliding glass door in the den and stare out over the moonlit water until he spotted the barest hint of a silhouette on the horizon.

He judged the vessel to be around forty feet with the clear outline of a cabin. Probably a dual-engine cruiser with a hard top. The boat had appeared just hours after the second episode in his current podcast series had gone live. Exactly one week to the day after his initial interview with the retired Houston police detective.

His follow-up guest had been the sister of the seventh and final victim. Eileen Ballard had been eager for the interview and seemed to find solace in being able to speak at length about her sister's murder. She recalled in vivid detail the last time she'd seen her sister, what they'd talked about and what the victim had been wearing.

She always took such care with her clothing and makeup. I used to tease her that she'd been born in the wrong era. Our grandmother had left her a collection of vintage jewelry and accessories that she cherished. When she left for work that morning, she had on her favorite silk scarf. She'd tied it around her neck and pinned it to her dress with a silver brooch. They recovered the brooch with the body, but the scarf never turned up. I always found it odd that the killer took the time to unfasten the brooch only to leave it behind.

The memory floated away as Trent focused his gaze on the water. He hadn't placed much importance on the sightings at first. The presence of a boat on moonlit water seemed innocuous. Someone out night fishing or enjoying a midnight cruise. He couldn't even be sure it was the same vessel that returned night after night. But then he started paying attention to the routine. The boat always glided into his line of sight at precisely midnight. Stopped in the same location, establishing a pattern that he could no longer deny. Someone was out there watching the shoreline. Watching his house.

On the one night when the cruiser failed to appear, Trent had taken his neighbor's boat out for a close encounter. Rocking on the waves, he'd kept watch for well over an hour, but the phantom vessel never showed. After that, he remained onshore, observing from his window or the patio as a dark premonition had started to creep in with the mist.

Picking up his phone, he counted down the seconds to midnight. *Three, two, one...* He set the phone aside and scanned the horizon. There it was. Sailing across the glassy water like a ghost ship. Like a figment of his imagination. Each night, edging a bit closer to the shoreline, or so it seemed from his vantage.

He lifted his night-vision binoculars and trained the lenses on the horizon. Even with the aid of thermal imaging, he'd never been able to detect anyone onboard, much less make out a name on the hull. The vessel really did seem to be a mirage, but the icy suspicion that tingled his scalp was all too real.

That same chill feathered along his bare arms as he skimmed the boat from stem to stern. *Who are you? What the hell are you doing out there?*

A movement near the cabin caught his attention and adrenaline pulsed. Never before had he detected even a slight movement. The boat came and went as if guided by an invisible hand. Not tonight, though. As he peered through the eyepiece, a human form took shape.

Was he seeing things? He glanced away, blinked and refocused.

Still there.

As if somehow intuiting Trent's doubt, the figure moved out of the shadows and stepped boldly into the moonlight so there could be no mistaking his presence. But he kept his head turned away as if he knew someone would be watching. This new development puzzled and intrigued Trent even as his trepidation deepened. For the longest time, he remained fixated on the silhouette. He couldn't make out even grainy features from this distance.

Minutes ticked by before he set aside the binoculars and got up to stride down to the water's edge. The surf swirled around his ankles as he stood gazing out toward the cruiser. *Come on, you bastard. Tell me to my face what you want.* He thought about waving the vessel ashore, but that might be an invitation he'd soon regret.

The night was so quiet he imagined he could detect the low idle of the inboard motors. He could definitely hear the quieter tinkle of the wind chimes that hung from a neighbor's boathouse. He waded out, letting the water rise to his thighs and then to his waist before he dove under and resurfaced neck-deep. The cruiser remained stationary in the face of his dare, pitching on the waves before the prow finally turned toward the open water. Within minutes the boat had disappeared in the darkness.

Trent's gaze remained glued to the spot, then he abruptly returned to shore. He started walking with no destination in mind. Past the tinkling chimes. Past rickety docks with bobbing boats. Past a long line of darkened houses. A few minutes earlier, he'd wanted nothing so much as to crawl between cool sheets and close his eyes. Now he was too keyed up to sleep. Something had been nagging at him ever since the boat had first appeared on the horizon a week ago. *He knows who you are and where you live. He knows you're looking for him.*

An elusive monster that preyed on young women.

The Seaside Strangler.

The name sounded like something from a low-budget horror movie, which had been the point. He'd wanted to grab attention for his podcast series. Mission accomplished, if the mysterious boat was any indication. In hindsight, the moniker seemed a little too contrived and not really apt since the murders had taken place in seven different communities, including Houston. Still, if Trent was right, the killer had ties to this town. In a sense, the *strangler* in him had been born here. For whatever reason, he'd been resurrected. To find him, Trent needed the help of a certain police detective who found herself in a place he'd been three years ago. A blue-eyed blonde who had the reputation of being impulsive, reckless and tough as nails.

What makes you think you can trust her? She turned on you once. How do you know she won't do it again?

"I don't trust her," he muttered.

He didn't trust anyone. But Sydney Shepherd was the only cop he knew willing to put herself on the line no matter the consequences. She was still inexperienced as a detective. Not the partner he would have chosen if he had his pick, but she possessed something no one else had—access to her late father's records. One way or another, Trent intended to get inside that storage unit. Her cooperation would make things easier, but a refusal wouldn't stop him.

Scouring the empty horizon one last time, he returned home and put away his gear. Then he made the rounds through the bungalow, pausing in his office to scan the whiteboard he'd picked up from a junk shop. He followed a trail of blue x's all up and down the map of the I-45 corridor. The blue marks signified the seven original murders. A small cluster of three red x's indicated where the bodies of the three recent victims had been found—all in or near Seaside. Radiating from each of the marks was a series of intersecting lines and spirals that would appear chaotic and meaningless to the untrained eye, but to Trent they represented days and nights of painstaking research in order to establish even the smallest connection among the victims, past and present.

He studied the board, moving sticky notes like chess pieces until everything started to blur. Turning out the light in his office, he went down the hallway to his bedroom, collapsing on the mattress with a heavy sigh. He threw an arm over his eyes and slept.

A noise roused him sometime later. He swung his legs over the side of the bed and sat with his ear cocked toward the hallway, listening intently to the familiar night sounds. He heard nothing out of the ordinary, and yet the hair at the back of his neck lifted.

Easing the nightstand drawer open, he removed a weapon and rose to slip across the room to the door. He navigated down the narrow hallway, instinctively avoiding the creak-

ing floorboards in the center. He checked the front door first
and then went from room to room, methodically searching
every corner and closet and peering through windows and
out the back door. Nothing seemed amiss.

Satisfied that no one had invaded his sanctuary, he returned the firearm to the nightstand drawer and went out
to the kitchen for a glass of water. He stood staring out the
window over the sink as he drank. The moon was up, illuminating his neglected garden and the weed-strewn path-
way that led down to the water. He could still hear the faint
tinkle from the boathouse. For a moment, he imagined a
shoulder brushing against the chimes and then a hand lifting to silence them. Maybe he shouldn't have been so quick
to put away his weapon, he thought, and then shrugged off
his lingering unease. *No one's there.*

But even as he turned back toward the bedroom, another
sound halted him. He eased through the tiny foyer and
peered through the glass panes out to the porch. Then he
turned the dead bolt and jerked open the door. His neighbor's orange tabby darted up the porch steps and shot past
him into the house.

Already on edge, Trent jumped at the unexpected intrusion, then swore. Closing the door, he turned with another muttered oath. Larry had jumped up on the armchair
he'd claimed for himself when Trent had first moved in.
From the start, the tabby had made himself at home. Sometimes he'd curl up for a snooze while Trent edited videos or
watched TV. The cat never remained inside for more than
an hour or two at a time. He seemed to know better than
to overstay his welcome, which was far more intuitive than
most humans Trent knew.

Rather than settling down in his usual spot on the cush-
ion, Larry perched on the arm and began to yowl and paw

frantically at whatever the neighbor's granddaughter had tied around his neck. The kid had a penchant for torturing the poor cat, though not maliciously. She merely wanted to dress Larry up like one of her dolls, much to his chagrin. He'd once turned up on Trent's porch with a pearl necklace wound around his throat.

"Take it easy," Trent murmured as he knelt beside the chair. "What's she done to you this time?" The cat batted Trent's hand when he tried to unfasten the knot. "Do you want my help or don't you?"

He finally managed to remove the scarf from the distraught feline's neck, and then he took a moment to examine the fabric. He was no expert, but even he recognized the quality of the silk and the name of the designer stitched unobtrusively into the hem. The scarf looked old but well preserved except for a small brown stain that covered two tiny holes. Recognition niggled.

Leaving Larry to his leisurely bath, Trent headed down the hallway to his office, where he plopped down behind his computer and opened an audio file. The interview with Eileen Ballard was still fresh on his mind, but he had to be sure—

There it was. The description of the dead woman's scarf. *Navy with swirls of green, pink and yellow.* It had been pinned around the victim's neck when she left for work that morning. She hadn't come home that night. Five days later, her body had been discovered in an abandoned warehouse in Houston. She was still fully clothed except for the missing scarf and her shoes.

Trent took a closer look at the stain. Blood? Possibly the victim's or the perpetrator's DNA? He folded the scarf almost reverently before slipping it into a protective bag.

A silk scarf belonging to a woman who'd been murdered

twenty years ago in Houston had turned up tied around a cat's neck in Seaside. Any humor or irony in the absurd situation was lost on Trent. Any doubt he had as to the occupant of the mysterious boat vanished.

The killer was back. And he wanted to play.

Chapter Three

Sydney was released from the hospital the following afternoon. She'd been dressed and ready to go since early that morning. The lieutenant had called at nine to see if she needed a ride home, but she declined his offer. She wasn't yet ready to face him after the way they'd ended things the day before. His voice on the phone had sounded stilted, and their conversation was so strained that she found herself ending the call without mentioning the visit from Gabriel Mathison.

For as long as she could remember, Dan Bertram had been a constant in her life—a mentor, a champion and sometimes a confidant. Someone she could always count on to have her best interests at heart. But her recent behavior had caused him to lose confidence in her. If she told him that Mathison had shown up in her hospital room in the dead of night, he might suspect she was lying to prove a point. Worse than that, she'd begun to doubt herself. A part of her wondered if she'd dreamed Gabriel Mathison at her bedside. If his threats had been nothing more than a feverish hallucination brought on by trauma and painkillers.

One thing was certain. She hadn't imagined the white roses. She read the card a few times, trying to figure out who had sent them. Finally coming to the conclusion that the Mathisons were playing mind games with her, she asked the nurse to give the flowers to another patient.

While she waited for her release papers, she practiced walking up and down the hallway on crutches. Every part of her body screamed for relief, but she ignored the aches and pains. The sooner she became mobile, the sooner she could get back to work. The prospect of sitting in her apartment and doing nothing for the next six weeks made her anxious. Already she had cabin fever after a single night in the hospital. However, by the time the attendant wheeled her downstairs to the waiting car service, her muscles trembled from exhaustion, and home had never sounded better.

Sunday afternoon traffic was light. She checked her messages on the ride to her apartment and then stared out the window until the car turned down her block. At her direction, the driver pulled all the way to the end of the driveway. He got out and opened the door for her, then held her crutches while she awkwardly disembarked.

"You live up there?" He nodded to the garage apartment. "Are you sure you can climb the stairs?"

She wasn't at all sure, but she gave him a confident nod. "Yeah, no worries. I've got this." She waited until he backed out of the driveway before clomping over to the steps, pausing at the bottom to psyche herself up for the climb. She tried to remember the advice she'd been given before she left the hospital. Weight concentrated on her hands, lead with her good foot going up.

"Need some help?"

She'd been so deep in concentration that the male voice, seemingly coming from nowhere, startled her. She jumped, dropped a crutch and had to grab onto the banister to keep from toppling over.

Her first assumption was that her landlord had come out

to check on her. He was a quiet, solitary man who spent most of his days reading on his patio or working in his garden. He spoke when spoken to, but other than the necessary conversations regarding repairs and upkeep, he left Sydney to her own devices, which suited her fine.

Rather than the older Martin Swann, however, the man who emerged from the overgrown hedge looked to be in his early to midthirties, tall and fit with wavy black hair and the most extraordinary blue eyes Sydney had ever looked into. The irises were so vivid, in fact, she thought he must surely wear tinted contacts to enhance them.

He lifted a hand in a friendly wave, and the smile he flashed was utterly disarming. Sydney gawked, then caught herself and closed her mouth. Since when had she become so susceptible to a handsome face? She decided to blame the concussion.

"You startled me," she said with a frown.

"I'm sorry." He crossed the narrow expanse of grass. "I saw you through the bushes. You seemed to have difficulty getting out of the car. I thought you might need a hand."

"Thank you, but I'm fine." Balancing on one foot, she leaned down for the crutch. Who the heck was he, anyway? And what business did he have spying on her? The thought crossed her mind that he might have been hired by Richard Mathison to keep an eye on her. Or worse, harass her in some way. Maybe she was being paranoid, but his own son had warned her the worst was yet to come.

"Here, let me get that for you. It's the least I can do." He closed the distance between them and bent to retrieve the crutch. Clinging to the banister, Sydney gave him a careful inspection while his head was lowered. A line she'd read somewhere came to mind: *Beware the tall, dark stranger.*

He straightened and handed her the crutch, squinting

past her up the stairs. "Not to be a pessimist, but those steps look pretty steep. Are you sure you can manage?"

"I guess we'll find out." Now that she had both crutches tucked underneath her arms, she was starting to regain her equilibrium. There was something about the stranger that rang a faint bell. She was certain they'd never met—who could forget those eyes?—yet he seemed vaguely familiar. She couldn't put her finger on why. "You said you saw me through the hedge?" An accusatory note crept into her tone as she continued to observe him.

He looked sheepish, as if he'd been caught with his hand in the proverbial cookie jar. "Yes, sorry. I know how that must sound, but I swear I wasn't being nosy on purpose. I heard the car and thought it might be my uncle. I'm still getting used to the comings and goings around here." He motioned over his shoulder to the row of oleanders. "I just moved in a few days ago. I'm Brandon, by the way. Brandon Shaw."

"Sydney Shepherd. What happened to Mrs. Dorman?"

"Who?"

She lifted a brow. "The previous owner? Nice elderly lady with white hair?"

"Oh, *that* Mrs. Dorman." He slid his hands in his pockets and rocked back with a quick grin. "The name didn't ring a bell at first. I've never actually met the woman."

"Then how did you end up in her house?" She wondered if she sounded as suspicious to him as she did to her own ears. Normally, she wouldn't have cared, but she didn't want to scare him off until she figured out whether or not he had a connection to the Mathisons.

He didn't seem to mind the question. He answered with an easygoing shrug. "She was called away on a family emergency. Something about a sister in Florida having hip surgery. She'll be gone for several weeks at least. Uncle

Marty knew that I was looking for a quiet place near the water for the summer. He suggested a short-term lease, and Mrs. Dorman agreed. The arrangement works well for both of us. I'm less than ten minutes from the marina, and she has someone looking out for her place while she collects a rent check to help with expenses."

A perfectly logical explanation, but Sydney still wasn't convinced. In her experience, someone who looked like Brandon Shaw didn't just appear out of the blue. "You keep referring to your uncle. You don't mean Martin Swann, do you?"

"Yes. Why does that surprise you?"

"I wasn't aware he had any family. I've lived here for nearly two years, and I've never known him to have a single visitor." She thought of the older man bent over his tasks in the garden, seemingly oblivious to the rest of the world. She'd always felt a bit sorry for him, although she wasn't sure why. She was alone, too, and she frequently reminded herself that was how she liked it.

"I suppose I'm the last of his family." Brandon Shaw fell silent for a moment as he glanced back over his shoulder toward Martin's patio. "We aren't blood relatives, but he was like a surrogate uncle to me when I was a kid. We lost touch for many years after my family moved away. When we finally reconnected, I was surprised to see how much he'd changed. He's grown older, of course. And sadder, I think. I don't know that he ever got over losing his wife. The Uncle Marty from my childhood was gregarious and playful. We used to follow him around like little lost puppy dogs."

"We?"

A frown played across his brow as he nodded toward the house next door. "My siblings and I. We lived here when we were children. It's strange being back on my own. I thought there might be ghosts, but no. It's just a house."

"You grew up in Seaside?"

"I wish," he said with a sigh. "We were only here for a short time, but this place made an impression. I've always wanted to come back and spend more time here."

"Well, I hope it lives up to your memories." Despite her reservations, he intrigued her. Had their paths crossed as children? Was that why he seemed familiar? "It's a nice place to vacation if you don't mind the quiet."

"The quiet is one of the best things about it. But I don't think of my time here as a vacation. Not in the usual sense. It's more of a hiatus," he explained. "A necessary pause from my regular routine to recharge and regroup. I was burned out with my work and a little depressed in the city. The constant whir of activity can start to wear you down. Not to mention the noise. Jackhammers and blaring horns everywhere you go. So loud you can't think. So much smog and exhaust you can't breathe. After a while, you become numb to the chaos…"

He trailed off, as if he'd shared more than he'd intended. He tried to downplay his revelations with another quick shrug. "Anyway, a friend suggested a change of scenery, and I immediately thought of this place. It's a short drive away if I need to get back, and the slower pace is just what I've been craving. Unfortunately, I'd already committed to teaching a summer writing course, but other than that, I don't plan to do anything for the next few weeks except fish and swim."

"Oh, you're a writer," Sydney said. "That's interesting."

"I dabble a bit. You know what they say about those who can't." His self-deprecating smile turned knowing. "Any other questions I can answer for you?"

She tried to look contrite. "Sorry. I didn't mean to give you the third degree."

"Force of habit, I would imagine. You're a police detective, right?" He placed a foot on the bottom step and leaned against the banister. "Marty mentioned you'd be my neighbor. Imagine my surprise when I heard your name on the local news this morning. They showed a photograph of the car you were driving. An unmarked sedan, the best I could tell."

"You're very observant."

"And you're lucky to be alive."

"That seems to be the consensus."

He glanced up the steps once again. "So, those stairs…"

She drew a breath and released it. "Yes. The stairs."

"Tell you what. I'll follow you up. If you lose your balance, I'll catch you."

"Or I'll knock you down and we'll both break our necks."

"There is that," he agreed. "I'm willing to risk it."

Sydney's internal alarm sounded again. Why was he going out of his way to be so helpful? Was she that jaded? Had she lost the ability to accept an act of kindness at face value? The answer was yes. She was exactly that jaded. "Thank you, but I couldn't ask you to do that," she protested. "I've taken up too much of your time as it is."

"I have nothing but time." He motioned toward the stairs. "Shall we?"

She didn't see how she could gracefully refuse, so she turned and gripped her crutches. *Weight on your hands, lead with your good foot. Check your balance before moving on to the next step.*

"Steady as she goes," he echoed. "One step at a time. Nice and slow…"

The climb was torturous. Sydney liked to think of herself as decently in shape. She ran. She trained. She took the occasional Pilates class. But by the time she reached the top step, she was breathing hard and her muscles quivered. She stepped onto the narrow wraparound landing and leaned against the wall to steady her balance. "That was even harder than I thought it would be."

"You'll get the hang of it," he said cheerfully. "Going down might be a bit daunting at first."

"I'll cross that bridge when I come to it." Propping one crutch against the wall, she searched through her bag for a house key rather than retrieving the one she kept hidden beneath a flower pot. Brandon Shaw might be a genuinely nice person, and the fact that Martin Swann knew him personally helped to ease her mind, but he was still a stranger, and sometimes the person with the easiest smile concealed the darkest secrets.

"May I?" He took the key from her hand, turned the lock and pushed open the door for her. Then he dropped the key in her palm and moved back to the top of the stairs as if to let her know he didn't expect—or even want—to be invited inside.

"Thanks again for your help."

"Anytime. I mean that. If you need anything, just let me know."

He went down a few steps before turning to glance back up at her. "Something just occurred to me. It seems you'll have a lot of time on your hands for the next few weeks, and I'm guessing you're not a binge-watcher. If you get bored, you can always check out my writing class. I post new lectures on Tuesday and I live stream every Thursday evening at seven. The chat section can get pretty lively, especially when I read aloud from class assignments. Just hit the notification bell so you'll be alerted when I upload."

"I'll check them out, but I won't be able to contribute," she said. "I don't know anything about writing."

"That's the point of taking a class, isn't it? To learn something new? You might surprise yourself. I'll wager there's more than a story or two inside your head. Just give it some thought. If you get bored."

"I'll think about it." She shifted her weight on the crutches, wanting nothing more than to retreat inside. She needed to rest and elevate her foot. She needed a shower and some food. She needed to be alone. The past twenty-four hours had taken a mental and physical toll. Her ankle hurt, her head hurt, her bruised rib hurt. Not to mention her ego. On top of all that, she'd probably lost a career she loved. Police work was all she'd ever wanted to do. What was she supposed to do now?

For some reason, Trent Gannon popped into her head. If anyone could understand her angst at the moment, it would be him.

She was readying her excuse to disappear inside when the back gate slammed shut, and they both glanced down the driveway in unison. Martin Swann stood on the pavement gazing back at them. He clutched a large box in his arms. Unlike Brandon Shaw, her landlord would never be noticed in a crowd. His appearance was completely non-descript from his pressed khaki pants to his crisp button-down shirt. Yet there was the gleam of curiosity and keen intelligence behind his wire-rimmed glasses.

His gaze darted from Sydney to Brandon, then back to Sydney. "I'm glad I caught you." He shifted the box to his hip. "I heard about the accident. Are you okay? You weren't seriously hurt?"

"A little banged up, but I'll live."

"I'm so relieved to hear it." He seemed to remember the

package and hurried over to the stairs. "This came for you yesterday. The delivery service left it on my front porch."

"Must be my new printer, judging by the size of the box."

"People still use printers?" Brandon teased.

"You might be surprised how often," she said.

"It's bulky." Martin shifted the weight yet again. "Shall I bring it up for you?"

"Let me save you the trouble." Before Sydney could utter a word, Brandon Shaw breezed down the stairs and took the box from Martin. His back was to Sydney. She couldn't hear the exchange between the two men, but Martin looked annoyed before he relinquished the box and lifted his gaze to Sydney.

"I'm glad you're okay," he said.

She nodded. "Thank you. And thank you for bringing over my delivery."

Brandon bounded up the steps with the oversized package as if it weighed no more than an ounce or two. The thought crossed Sydney's mind that he'd done it on purpose just to flaunt his youth and vitality in the older man's face. But she didn't know either man well enough to make such a judgment.

"Where do you want it?" Brandon asked.

"What? Oh, you can just leave it here on the porch," Sydney said. "I'll take it in later."

"Are you sure? I'm already here, willing and able."

Again, he was so friendly and accommodating she could hardly refuse. "All right. Just put it inside the door if you don't mind."

"Not at all." He pushed open the door with his hip and disappeared inside.

She glanced down the steps where Martin Swann still waited as if he expected her to say or do something. Normally, he was the one who broke off their brief exchanges. She gave him a wave. "Thanks again."

He turned without another word and walked back toward his gate.

She left the door open when she went inside. Brandon had placed the box on the floor and was now surveying her place with unabashed curiosity. "It's smaller than I remembered."

"You've been here before?" she asked in surprise.

"Years ago. It wasn't an apartment back then. Uncle Marty used the space as a kind of den. A man cave, if you will. He would come up here when his wife had her bridge parties in the main house. She was a lot more social than Marty. He got on far better with us kids than he did with adults." He looked momentarily lost in memories. "A friend and I used to sneak up here when Marty was at work or out of town and pretend the place was our clubhouse. We even left our initials inside the bedroom closet. But I'm sure that wall has been painted over many times since then."

"No initials that I've noticed." Sydney hovered just inside the door.

He didn't take the hint, but instead he crossed the room and glanced out the window that overlooked the backyard and pool area next door. His eyes glinted when he turned. "That's quite a view. No skinny-dipping for me."

"Your pool, your rules." She moved aside to give him room to exit. "Thanks again for your help."

"It was my pleasure." He grinned as he moved past her through the door. "Don't forget about the writing class. Just do a search on my name. The videos should pop up."

"I'll remember." She followed him out to the porch and watched as he descended the stairs, glad to see the last of him but admiring and envying his agility at the same time.

When he got to the bottom, he glanced over his shoulder with another smile. "See you soon, Sydney."

SEE YOU SOON, SYDNEY.

The expression was common. People said it all the time. Just another way to communicate "goodbye" or "so long" or "take care." But she had a hard time believing that particular wording was a coincidence. First the anonymous message that came with the roses, then Gabriel Mathison whispering in her ear. Now a stranger uttering the exact same catchphrase from the bottom of her steps.

Her suspicions were triggered enough that she decided to run a background check on Brandon Shaw. She opened her laptop to log into the department's database. Password denied. She repeated the process until the system locked her out for too many false tries. She stared at the screen in frustration even as she reminded herself that limiting access during a suspension was protocol. But someone— probably the lieutenant—had certainly acted fast, maybe because he had reason to believe she wasn't coming back.

Or he knew she wouldn't sit around twiddling her thumbs for the next six weeks.

What was she supposed to do? It wasn't like she enjoyed prying into someone's personal business, but her new neighbor was just a little too perfect, a little too helpful and his arrival next door a little too timely. Maybe he was exactly who he seemed—an uncommonly handsome man looking to escape the pressures and intrusions of the modern world—but that little voice in her head reminded her that appearances were often deceiving.

She couldn't run a background check, but she could certainly talk to her landlord. She would be very interested in hearing Martin's take on their past. Would his recollection corroborate Brandon Shaw's story, or would his memories destroy a carefully fabricated life? Something about the younger man's account didn't quite ring true. Maybe she was being cautious to the point of paranoia, but she'd be a fool not to take Mathison's threats seriously. *Sometimes when you think someone is out to get you, they really are out to get you.*

Still reflecting on the encounter, she closed and locked the door, then hobbled over to the window to glance out. She'd always admired Mrs. Dorman's shady backyard and pool area. Like Martin, the older woman spent most of her time outdoors. Gardening seemed more of a passion that a pastime. She was fastidious in her upkeep. Would she really abandon her beloved flowers for the entire summer? Did she even have a sister in Florida?

Okay, now you really do sound paranoid. Take a pain pill and chill.

She did neither. Instead, she lingered at the window, searching the shadowy corners of the yard and peering into the sunroom. The blinds were up, but the bright daylight allowed her a glimpse into the space. She detected no sign of life inside or outside the house. Maybe he'd stopped by to visit with Martin. If they'd been as close as he'd insinuated earlier, they probably had a lot of catching up to do.

But what about that odd moment over the printer box? Had she imagined the sudden tension? She wasn't in a good place. Pain and trauma could too easily alter a person's perception. Already, she could feel the gossamer tentacles of obsession starting to latch on. She told herself to let it go. Focus on something else. But she couldn't. She kept coming back to that brief moment at the bottom of the steps. Maybe Martin wasn't all that happy to have a surrogate nephew turn up in his life after so many years. Maybe their past hadn't been quite as harmonious as Brandon would have her believe.

With a little muscle and a lot of determination, she managed to scoot her dad's old recliner next to the window. She'd be able to keep an eye on the house next door while remaining inconspicuous behind the blinds. Not to mention keeping her foot elevated. When she had the recliner positioned, she dragged over a side table to hold her laptop, remote and all the other paraphernalia she would need to keep herself occupied. She fussed until she had the niche just so, then she went through the apartment rolling up throw rugs and relocating items on the floor that might trip her up in the middle of the night.

By the time she finished, she'd worked up a sweat. Pulling a plastic cast cover over her ankle, she managed to take a shower and wash her hair. Every little task required prodigious effort and seemed to take forever. Climbing over the side of the tub without falling. Balancing on one foot to dry off. Finding a pair of sweatpants loose enough to slip over her cast.

Hobbling back into the living room, she abandoned the idea of a late lunch and headed straight for the recliner. Exhaustion claimed her within minutes, and she fell into a deep sleep with her ankle propped up on the footrest and her head nestled against the worn leather.

She dreamed. Not about the Mathisons or Brandon Shaw or Martin Swann, though the strange quartet had certainly drifted in and out of her thoughts for the past twenty-four hours. She dreamed about Trent Gannon. She literally hadn't thought of him in years, and like a bad penny, he'd turned up at the hospital when she was at her worst. When she desperately needed someone in her corner whether she wanted to admit it or not.

Did she trust him? No. Maybe he really had managed to let go of an old grudge, but he definitely had an agenda. She gave him credit for owning up to the real reason he'd come to see her.

Her cell phone startled her awake. For a moment, she hadn't a clue where she was. The pain medication made her groggy and disoriented. She felt momentary panic until the familiar sounds and scents enveloped her, and she sighed in relief. She was home.

The ringtone pealed again. She tried to blink away the cobwebs as she glanced at the screen. The number was unfamiliar. She started to let the call go to voicemail, then decided it might be important. She pressed the Accept button and put the phone on speaker.

"Hello?" Using the lever on the side of the chair, she adjusted the back to a sitting position.

"Are you watching the press conference?"

She frowned at the phone. "Who is this?"

"Trent Gannon."

Trent Gannon. Bad penny, indeed. "How did you get my number?"

"A mutual friend."

"What friend?"

He ignored the question. "Turn on channel four."

"Why? What's going on?" She used the remote to turn on the flat-screen. When Richard Mathison's face appeared in her living room, she bolted upright. "Is this from yesterday's press conference?"

"No, it's live outside city hall right now. You're just catching the end of it. Hold on a second." She could hear the blare of his television in the background until he muted the sound. "He's not taking questions, apparently. Just reading from a prepared script. The guy on the left is one of his attorneys."

"He looks formidable," Sydney muttered.

"Exactly the reaction he'd want you to have."

She tried to dispel the feeling of doom that had settled over the room with the appearance of Richard Mathison on her TV screen. "What did he say? Mathison, I mean."

"You're not going to like it," Trent warned.

She clutched the arm of the chair. "Just tell me."

"He's threatening a major lawsuit against the Seaside PD for misconduct, harassment, endangerment and a host of other grievances. His attorneys are prepared to file the paperwork by the end of the week unless they can reach an agreement with the department."

"What are they asking for?"

"Your head on a platter, basically. They want you fired."

Her heart sank. "Mathison actually said that? He used my name?"

"He claims you acted irrationally, recklessly and in a manner unbecoming to your profession and to your community. He wants to make an example of you."

She leaned back against the leather and closed her eyes. What would her father say if he could see her now? His record had been exemplary to the very end of his career. He'd been an asset to the department and a true hero to the community. She was almost relieved that he wasn't around to witness her epic downfall.

I blew it, Dad.

Then own it, Syd. Make it right no matter what it takes.

Okay, but how was she supposed to do that, exactly?

"You still there?"

"Yeah." She turned her head to the window, staring down into the garden next door.

Trent's voice softened unexpectedly. "Are you okay?

Maybe I shouldn't have been so blunt. Tact has never been my thing."

She sighed. "It's not like I haven't been expecting it. The suspension was just the first step. In all honesty, my career was probably over the moment I took on the Mathisons."

"But you did it anyway. That took guts."

She winced. "I did my job. Poorly, as it turns out. My actions were anything but courageous."

"I disagree." He was quiet for a moment. "This probably won't mean much to you at the moment, but I have a pretty good idea of how you're feeling."

She appreciated the sentiment, but his commiseration didn't help at all. Different detectives, different circumstances. Then she chided herself for making the distinction. She was hardly in a position to feel superior. She hadn't shown up intoxicated to a crime scene, but some might argue that her actions had been even more irresponsible and dangerous.

"I'm glad you told me," she said. "And for the record, you don't have to walk on eggshells around me. I can handle bluntness. What I can't abide is someone using weasel words to let me down easy. Or mislead me."

"Fair enough. I don't know if what I'm about to say falls under that category or not, but I would remind you that you haven't been fired yet. There's always a possibility the powers that be will call Mathison's bluff."

"A very slim possibility. Aren't you the one who warned me about circling wagons?"

"Yes, but you have something I didn't have when I came up against the machine. You have a decorated lieutenant with clout and seniority in your corner."

"You mean Dan Bertram. Even if he's still on my side— which is a very big if at this point—I don't want him risking his career for me." She tucked a pillow underneath her foot. Her ankle had started to throb again. She reached for the bottle on the side table and gulped a pain pill without water. "What else did Mathison say?"

"Actually, he presented an interesting theory," Trent told her. "He brought up the two unsolved homicides from last year that you were keen to pin on Gabriel Mathison."

"I wasn't *keen* to pin anything on him," she said. "I looked into the possibility of a connection based on the killer's MO."

"Sorry. Poor choice of words. Anyway, Mathison claims the police department allowed you to scapegoat his son in an effort to distract from their incompetence and corruption."

"Wow," she said in surprise. "He's throwing the whole department under the bus. So much for his friendship with the chief. I wonder what she thinks about this press conference."

"You can bet every word he utters has been vetted and serves an agenda. He insists the police knew all three murders are connected but they withheld the information from the public."

"Wait. He *admitted* the murders are connected?"

"Don't get too excited," Trent cautioned. "Remember what I said about every word serving an agenda. According to him, Jessica King's law firm represents one of the most powerful drug kingpins in this part of the state. If she came across information that legally bound her to notify the authorities, then her murder was likely a professional hit. Mathison says the police department has known about the drug link all along but have been threatened or bribed into holding their silence while allowing you to harass his son."

"*I* harassed *him*? That's a good one," she muttered. "I researched Jessica's law firm. They're well respected. I never saw or heard anything that suggested a nefarious clientele."

"That's not something they'd advertise. But I take it you're not buying Mathison's theory."

"It's just a smokescreen," she said in frustration. "He's being deliberately misleading. I agree the cases are related, but I think Gabriel Mathison is the missing link, not some two-bit drug lord."

"What if you're both wrong?"

That stopped her cold. "You still think a killer who disappeared twenty years ago has suddenly become active again?"

"Put it this way. The probability that I'm onto something is a lot higher today than it was yesterday."

"Why?"

"There's been a new development. I would call it significant."

"What's the development?"

"It'll take some explaining," he said. "I'd rather we meet in person."

"That's problematic for me." She lifted her foot as if he could see the effort. "In case you forgot, I'm not exactly mobile at the moment."

"I'll come to you, then. What's the address?"

Was she in the mood for company? Not really. The pain pill was already starting to take effect. She could easily close her eyes and drift back to sleep, but the prospect of spending an hour or two with Trent Gannon didn't sound half bad. If nothing else, he'd be a distraction. Left to her own devices, she'd spend too much time napping and fretting.

She glanced at the phone, realizing Trent was still talking. "I'm sorry, what did you say?"

"I said the sooner we can meet, the better. I'd like to get your take on something that happened last night."

"Is it about the new development?"

"It's all related, but I should warn you up front, this could get hairy. Given your current physical limitations, I thought long and hard before calling you. This guy...this killer..." He paused. "If I'm right, he already knows who I am and where I live. Dragging you into this may not end well for either of us."

The pulse in her throat jumped. If anyone else had delivered such a grim caveat, she might have dismissed their concerns as melodramatic. But not Trent Gannon. She had a feeling he was just being blunt.

He misinterpreted her silence. "You've got a lot on your plate at the moment. Feel free to tell me to take a hike. That's what I'd do."

"No, you wouldn't."

"You don't know the whole story yet." She heard his chair squeak as he got up, probably to pace. "Before I say anything else, I need assurance that any involvement on your end will remain discreet. The last thing I want is to bring any kind of danger to your doorstep. Agreed?"

"You're serious about this."

"Dead serious."

She'd never been one to shy away from danger. Some would argue that she had a tendency to run headlong toward it. Whether that was a good thing or not remained to be seen. "As you said, given my current limitations, keeping a low profile is pretty much a necessity."

"This isn't just about going through your dad's files," he warned. "Although I'd still like to take a look at his notes whenever you're ready. To be brutally honest, I'm alone on this hunt. A fresh pair of eyes and ears could make all the difference."

"And you trust my input?" *Even after all my screwups? You really are desperate.* "Anything I can do to help."

He still sounded unsure. "In that case, let me give you something to mull over before we meet. Supposing those old cases really are connected to the more recent strangulations. Think about what I told you yesterday. Seven murders in seven years, then nothing. The trail went cold. Two decades later, three more bodies have been discovered in less than a year. What does that suggest?"

"He's not only active again, he's escalating from his old pattern. Assuming we're dealing with the same suspect."

"He's escalating and he's taking chances," Trent said. "No one else is looking for him. It's just us. If we don't pick up the trail soon, he'll kill again. He'll keep killing until we stop him. Or he stops us."

She rubbed the back of her neck where goose bumps still prickled. "In that case, you'd better come right over."

Chapter Four

After the call ended, Sydney sat in the recliner digesting Trent's information. The prospect of a new investigation excited her, but even as she jotted down a few notes from their conversation, a part of her had already started to question his true intent.

She wanted to believe he valued her skills and experience as a detective, but her suspension would suggest otherwise. Even on her best day, she still had a lot to learn. So why her?

Maybe the better question was, who else but her? He didn't have a lot of friends left in the department. Most had written him off a long time ago. Could his willingness to work with her be a simple matter of two discredited cops finding themselves out in the cold together?

Whatever his intent, she wasn't about to turn down the opportunity. Bringing an elusive killer to justice would be its own reward, but a part of her had already started to analyze the related benefits. A takedown of that magnitude could go a long way toward the rehabilitation of her reputation, particularly with Dan Bertram. It might even neutralize Richard Mathison's ultimatum and save her career.

Her thoughts chugged on in that hopeful vein as she hoisted herself out of the chair and reached for her crutches. Hobbling back into the bedroom closet, she searched the top shelf for a plastic bin containing a few of her father's possessions. Most everything else had been placed in storage, but she'd brought a few sentimental items to her apartment, including his detective shield and the revolver in her nightstand that had been passed down from her grandfather.

Using one of her crutches to drag the container to the edge of the shelf, she teetered on her good foot until she could grab the handles. Ignoring the pain in her injured ankle, she lowered herself to the floor and dug through the contents until she found the key to the storage unit. Then she spent the next few minutes sorting through the bin before removing a pair of binoculars her dad had kept in the trunk of his car for stakeouts.

Memories came flooding back as she looped the leather strap around her neck. She'd been all of twelve years old, hot and fidgety in a sweltering car as she sat with her dad outside an apartment complex waiting for a suspect to emerge. To keep her entertained, he'd lectured her on the finer points of stakeouts.

Without proper predicate, surveillance is nothing more than snooping. A violation of a basic right that should never be taken lightly. Since I'm off duty you might ask if what we're doing crosses a line. The answer is no, because of an exception called probable cause. I have reason to believe the suspect is engaged in illegal activity, so I need to keep track of his movements. You'll come across cops—maybe even someone you've known and admired in the past—who'll try to persuade you to ignore procedure for the sake of expediency, but that's not what we're about, okay? We follow the law. We observe protocol. Nothing comes back on us.

Then he'd walked her through the basics of wiretapping, trackers and a host of other surveillance devices that required warrants. Despite the heat and her discomfort, Sydney had hung on his every word. She'd thrilled to his use of "we," making it seem as if they were partners. Perched beside him on the front seat of his hot car, he'd seemed bigger than life, a hero to be admired and revered and emulated. And that was the very day she'd decided to follow in his footsteps.

She went back out to the living room and placed the binoculars on the end table beside the recliner. Computer, phone, notebook and now binoculars. *Quite the little spy nest you've built for yourself.* She felt a momentary prickle of guilt. Did she have the proper predicate to surveil her new neighbor? Did she have probable cause to keep track of his movements? Less than twenty-four hours ago, she'd been threatened by Gabriel Mathison. Then a stranger had turned up next door. A man who, by his own admission, had been watching her through the hedge. She had every right to be suspicious. She'd be a fool not to take precautions. For now, the spy nest stayed.

While she waited for Trent, she tidied up the place as best she could. Ten minutes later, she was just coming down the hallway when a knock sounded on the door.

"It's open!"

He came in balancing a paper bag and a drink tray in one hand. "I hope you don't leave your door unlocked all the time."

"I knew you were coming." She leaned on the crutches. "What's all this?"

"I didn't know if you'd eaten, so I stopped by a food truck on the way over. Two-for-one tacos. I hope you're hungry."

"Starving. I haven't been able to eat much since before the accident."

He gave her an admonishing look. "That's not good.

You'll need all the strength you can muster just to get around on those crutches. Speaking of...how are you managing?"

"I've had better days," she admitted.

"Sore?"

"You have no idea."

"I've had my share of bruised ribs, so I sympathize. Those stairs must have been fun."

She grimaced. "I don't look forward to my first trip down them."

"Sit and scoot would be my advice."

The banter was surprisingly companionable considering their acrimonious past and the fact they barely knew one another. Maybe their separate experiences in the hot seat had accelerated a comradery that would never have existed without their respective transgressions. Whatever the case, Sydney was glad she'd agreed to the meeting. If nothing else, Trent's visit beat an afternoon of wallowing in pain and self-pity.

He glanced around with unabashed curiosity. "So, this is your place. Not what I expected, but I like it."

She tried to imagine the apartment through his eyes. Small and sparsely furnished. *Utilitarian* was the word that came to mind. But the residential neighborhood of older homes suited her and the view through some of the windows, particularly at night, made her feel as if she were floating in the trees. "What did you expect?" she asked curiously.

He thought about it for a minute. "I guess I figured you for one of those modern places with all the amenities. Indoor swimming pool, coffee lounge, a big shiny workout room."

She glanced down at her sweatpants. "Really? That seems my speed to you?"

He shot her a quick grin. "I may have had preconceived notions about you based on our past experiences."

"At least you're willing to admit it." She followed his gaze around the space. "It may not look like much, but it suits me fine. The neighborhood is quiet. No one above, below or on either side of me."

"It's off the beaten track," he agreed. "How did you find this place anyway?"

"Someone posted an ad on the station bulletin board. I was actively looking for a new apartment, so it seemed like it was meant to be." She pointed to her tiny dining table when he held up the paper bag. "Over there." Then she instructed him where to find plates and napkins while she grabbed her notebook. Taking a seat, she scribbled the date on a blank page as she surreptitiously watched him move about her tiny kitchen. He was dressed much as he had been the day before. Worn jeans, sneakers and a T-shirt with a hardware store logo on the back. His attire could charitably be described as thrift store chic, but the worn clothing somehow suited him. He could seamlessly blend into a crowd, yet there was something about him that elicited a second look when you met him face-to-face.

If someone had told her twenty-four hours ago that she'd be sneaking second, third and fourth glances at Trent Gannon in her own apartment, she wouldn't have been able to fathom such an unlikely scenario. But here they were.

He came over to the table and sat down across from her. "Dig in. I can personally vouch for the food. A buddy of mine owns the truck. He and his wife do all the cooking. Good people. I usually end up eating there a few times a week."

Funny, she would never have thought of him as having buddies or even casual friendships. He gave off strong loner vibes, but maybe she was projecting her own pre-conceptions.

She unwrapped a taco. "We should get started. I took a pain pill earlier, so my concentration may start to fade at some point."

He gave her a quick assessment. "None of my business, but be careful with the pills they give you for pain. They're stronger than you might think. Take it from someone who knows."

Again, she wondered what had set him on a bad path before his departure from the department. "I'll take that under advisement," she said with a nod. "Do you mind if I ask a personal question?"

"Go for it."

"What happened three years ago?" She quickly added, "You don't have to answer if you don't want to."

A frown flickered. "No, I get it. If we're doing this together, you need to know I won't go off on a bender and leave you hanging." He reached for the container of green sauce but left it unopened. "I lost someone close to me. It wasn't sudden."

"I'm sorry."

He gave a brief nod. "Watching someone you love suffer day after day, month after month…" He trailed off. "Turned out, she was a lot stronger than I was. The most heroic person I've ever known. My actions were cowardly by comparison. I started having a drink in the hospital parking lot just to get up enough courage to go inside. Then a few drinks when I got home to get through the night. Next thing I knew, I was the cop who kept a flask in his desk."

The haunted look in his eyes made Sydney regret her question. She hadn't meant to open a wound that was obviously still raw. "People handle grief in different ways."

"People handle grief every day and manage not to throw away a career they love," he said. "I don't make excuses for myself."

"But you're okay now."

He shrugged. "I no longer drink and I never will again. But as far as being okay...that's a relative term."

"Don't I know it," she muttered. "Thank you for telling me."

"Like I said, you have a right to know who you're getting into bed with, so to speak. Is there anything you want to tell me?"

She thought about his question for a moment. "No, I think I'm good."

He grinned at that, seemingly falling back into their easy companionship. He drenched his taco in green sauce and scarfed it down in a few big bites. Then he pushed aside his plate and wiped his hands and mouth on a paper napkin. All this occurred while she was still assessing his revelation. Who was the woman he lost and what had she been to him?

"Hungry?" she asked in amusement.

"That'll tide me over so that I can talk while you eat. I'll try not to take up too much of your time. I know you need to rest."

"I've already had my fill of rest. I can only imagine my mood after six weeks of being cooped up in here. I'm glad you called. I'm still not sure how much help I can be, but—" she picked up her pen "—let's give it a go. Do you mind if I take notes?"

"Notes might help. The story is complicated and gets more so all the time. Lots of names, lots of individual investigations. I guess the best place to start is where I left off yesterday—my podcast interview with the retired HPD detective."

"I don't remember you mentioning his name."

"Doug Carter." He waited until she jotted it down, then said, "For the sake of clarity, I'll refer to the seven victims by the number in which they were murdered rather than by name. No disrespect intended. I don't mean to reduce their humanity to a number or statistic, but if I start throwing a bunch of names at you all at once, it'll make it that much harder to keep track. And chronology is important in this case. Chronology is everything. You'll see why as we go along."

"It's your story. You can tell it however you like." She sampled her taco while she waited for him to begin.

He gave a vague nod as if he were already deep in thought. "Doug Carter was the lead investigator on the seventh and final case. He put me in touch with the victim's sister, a woman named Eileen Ballard. Like Carter, she's worked tirelessly for the past two decades trying to keep her sister's murder in the public forefront. Countless interviews. Letters and phone calls by the hundreds if not thousands. She still haunts HPD headquarters every single week for an update on her sister's case."

"Have her efforts been successful?"

He sighed. "You know how that goes. Twenty years is a long time. People move on and forget. A fresh crime or catastrophe captures the public's attention. It was only by happenstance that I learned about her sister's case and the six previous murders from another podcaster. If Doug Carter hadn't agreed to an interview, I would have moved on, too."

"Or found someone else to talk to about the murders."

"I like to think so, but who knows? Anyway, I managed to book Eileen for my podcast a week ago last Friday, one week after the interview with Doug Carter. She was excellent. Smart, quick, articulate. Sympathetic without being maudlin."

"Where can I listen to these interviews?"

"I'll give you the links. According to Eileen, she and her sister were very close. They shared an apartment and made a point of sitting down to breakfast every morning before they left for work. Eileen recounted in great detail everything about their last morning together. What they talked about, what they ate, even her sister's outfit. Apparently, she had a collection of vintage scarves and jewelry that had belonged to their grandmother. She wore her favorite scarf that day and fastened it around her neck with a silver brooch. The brooch was found with the body, but the scarf was never recovered. I stress these details because that scarf will be important later," he said.

Sydney wiped her hands, then scribbled *scarf* in her notebook and underlined the word three times before glancing up. "Was the victim strangled with the scarf?"

"No. The bruising patterns were consistent with someone's hands around her throat. Thumbs like so, the killer facing her." He demonstrated in the air. "That, too, will be important."

A shiver went through Sydney as she made a note in the margin.

"Here's where the story gets really interesting," he said, "at least from my point of view. Several hours after the interview went live, something strange occurred at my place, although I didn't think much of it at the time."

Sydney leaned forward in anticipation. "What happened?"

"I have a house on the bay just south of here. I was sitting outside enjoying the breeze when I noticed a boat a hundred yards or so out from shore. The lights were off, but I could see the silhouette of the vessel in the moonlight.

It stopped directly out from my house, stayed for about twenty minutes and then headed back out toward the gulf. As I said, I didn't think much about it at the time. Could have been someone night fishing or someone up to a more nefarious pastime. Lots of drug activity in this area, as you well know. I went to bed and forgot about the incident. But the boat came back the next night and the next night and the next. Always precisely at midnight. Always stopping straight out from my house except for the one night when I took my neighbor's boat out to intercept. That was the only time he didn't show."

Sydney felt a stir of excitement in the pit of her stomach. This was getting good—or bad, depending on one's perspective. "You think he was watching you?"

"How else would he have known I was on the water?"

"Is there a chance this could all be a coincidence? How can you be sure it's even the same boat?"

"I'm sure."

She tended to believe him. He didn't strike her as someone prone to exaggeration or an overactive imagination— the opposite, in fact. And the pattern he'd laid out was hard to ignore. "Did you try again to intercept?"

"No, but I started to observe the vessel through a pair of night-vision binoculars. Even with an image intensifier, I could never detect any sign of life onboard. No movement whatsoever. He was that careful. Last night everything changed. He came out of the cabin and stood in the moonlight for a good ten minutes as if to make sure I saw him. As if he wanted me to know that he knew I was watching him."

"Could you make out his features?"

"He was too far out and he kept his face turned away. After the boat disappeared, I took a long walk and then went to bed. Something woke me up from a deep sleep. A sound. An instinct. You know that feeling when something isn't right. I got up and checked all around the house. The only thing I found was my neighbor's cat on the porch. That's not unusual. My house has become Larry's second home. He comes and goes at all hours."

"Larry?"

"A big orange tabby. As soon as I opened the door, he shot inside. He had something tied around his neck and was frantic to get it off. That's not unusual, either. My neighbor's granddaughter likes to pretend Larry is one of her dolls. When I was finally able to remove the scarf—"

"Scarf?"

He gave a brief nod. "A vintage silk scarf with bright splashes of color. Exactly like the one Eileen Ballard had described earlier during our interview."

Sydney's first impulse was to accept the revelation and run with it, but she forced herself to play devil's advocate. "That doesn't mean it's the same scarf. After so many years, I'd say the chances are extremely slim. Isn't it more likely that someone heard the podcast and decided to mess with you? You said the sister described the scarf in vivid detail."

"The chances of *that* are extremely slim," Trent countered. "It's the same scarf. I'd stake my life on it. For one thing, the designer on the label is long dead. You can't just go out and buy another scarf like it. I also found tiny holes in the silk where the brooch had been fastened, along with a small stain that could be blood from a pinprick."

"Let's assume it is the same scarf," Sydney said. "Why would he give you a piece of evidence that could incriminate him in at least seven homicides?"

"I've given that a lot of thought," Trent said. "Maybe it's ego. Maybe it's control. He's had a twenty-year hiatus, and now he wants someone to know that he's back."

"That seems a simplistic explanation."

"Not really. Do you know anything about the BTK Killer? He would sometimes go years between kills, leaving notes in the interim for the Wichita police so they would know he was still around. It gave him a feeling of superiority and control. When he was finally captured, he said the anticipation he experienced from stalking and planning helped to sustain him during his dormant periods."

"But why would the killer contact you?"

"I've wondered about that, too. It's possible, maybe even probable that he heard my podcast. My interest in the murders gives us a connection."

Sydney studied him for a moment as her thoughts raced. "Do you realize what you're saying?"

"I know exactly what I'm saying. If DNA can be lifted from the stain, then I could be the only person on the planet with the means of identifying a serial killer who went to ground two decades ago."

"You left out the most important part," she said. "He knows who you are and where you live."

His gaze locked onto hers. "I warned you it could get dangerous."

The tension in the room had become so palpable they both jumped when someone knocked on her door. Sydney's gaze flew to the entrance and then back to Trent. *At least I'm not the only one on edge.*

He scooted back his chair. "Do you want me to get that for you? Are you expecting someone?"

"No." She took a quick breath. "You don't think—"

"No one followed me here. I made certain."

"Sorry. I guess I'm a little spooked." She gave a shaky laugh. "As if a serial killer would come knocking on my door in broad daylight."

A SUNTANNED MAN wearing swim trunks and an unbuttoned shirt stood on the porch with one hand planted on the door-frame. Trent's first thought when he opened the door and saw the pose was *Who the hell is this guy?* His second impression was more disciplined. Somewhere in his thirties. Six feet or a little less. One sixty, one-sixty-five. Dark hair, blue eyes. No visible scars or tattoos, but memorable none-theless. Memorable and vaguely familiar.

The man looked equally surprised to see Trent at the door. He straightened with an affable smile that was meant to disarm but didn't. "Is Sydney here?"

Trent's response was blunt. "Who wants to know?"

"I'm her neighbor. Sorry for the interruption. I didn't realize she had company." Sydney clomped up to the door on her crutches and the stranger's smile broadened. "There you are. I apologize for dropping by like this."

"No, it's fine," she said. "What's up?"

He made a vague gesture toward the yard below. "I'm having a few people over for an impromptu pool party. We're cooking out. Nothing fancy. Just burgers and grilled vegeta-bles. I wondered if I could bring you a plate when everything is ready. Or better yet, you're welcome to join us if you like."

"That's a very nice offer, but we've got tons of leftovers from a late lunch. As to the pool party…" She stuck out her cast. "I don't think I'm up for that just yet."

"A raincheck, then?"

"Of course."

The man's attention had vectored in on Sydney from the moment she walked up to the door. No big mystery there. She was an attractive woman. But Trent detected some-thing in her response that intrigued him. Her expression and tone remained cordial, yet there was a subtle rigidity to her posture that made him think her guard had gone up. He wondered why.

If the neighbor noticed, he didn't let on. His benign expression never wavered. "If you change your mind later, just come on over. Both of you." His gaze slid back to Trent.

Sydney said quickly, "Oh, sorry. Trent Gannon, this is Brandon Shaw. He just moved in next door. Trent is…an old friend."

Her hesitation amused Trent. She obviously didn't know how to classify their relationship. It was a little complicated, he had to admit.

Brandon's gaze narrowed as he cocked his head. "You look familiar. Have we met?"

"I was wondering the same thing," Trent said. "Any chance you came through the Seaside Police Department prior to three years ago?"

"Is that a subtle way of asking whether or not I've ever been arrested?" He gave Sydney a wink.

Trent shrugged. "Not at all. You could have come in to pay a parking ticket."

"I've never been inside the Seaside Police Station or any police station, for that matter. In fact, I've only been in town a few days. Interesting that your mind would go there, though. Are you also a detective…Trent?"

"Yes, but I don't work for the police department."

"Private security?" That seemed to perk the man's interest. "As it happens, I might be in the market for a new security system."

"Doesn't Mrs. Dorman already have an alarm?" Sydney asked.

"It's an antiquated system. I don't think it's been activated in years. But I'm not worried about my stay here. I'm interested in an upgrade for my home in the city."

"I'm afraid I wouldn't be able to help you," Trent said. "My specialty is surveillance and background checks."

"Cheating spouses and insurance fraud, eh?"

"Among other things."

"I'll certainly keep that in mind." His eyes glinted as he turned back to Sydney. "If you need anything, you know where to find me."

"Thank you again."

He started to exit, then pivoted. "See you both soon, I hope."

Trent waited until the man had bounded down the steps, then he closed the door and turned. "What's the deal with that guy?"

"What do you mean?"

He searched her features. "Maybe I'm wrong, but I thought you seemed tense. Any particular reason why?"

"We only just met today. It's my nature to be cautious around people I don't know. Including you," she added.

"As well you should be," Trent said, unoffended. "But what I sensed was more than a vague misgiving. What's going on?"

She gave him a sidelong glance as she moved away from the door. "Was it really that obvious?"

"I told you, I'm good at reading people. But don't worry. I doubt it would ever occur to your neighbor that anyone he encounters is less than bowled over by his looks and presence. Still, I'd be careful with that guy. If he senses your resistance, he might take it as a challenge."

Her tone was dismissive. "He can take it however he wants. I know how to shut down unwanted attention." She maneuvered over to the window and glanced out. "Besides, I don't think any interest he has in me is romantic or even personal."

"Meaning?"

She hesitated. "I really hadn't planned to get into this right now. We have other things to discuss, and besides, you'll just think I'm paranoid."

"Now you have to tell me."

She sat down on the arm of an old recliner, placing her back to the window as she propped her crutches against the side of the chair. In her baggy sweatpants and tank top, with the cuts and scratches from the accident still fresh on her face and arms, she looked almost fragile, though Trent suspected she would take exception to that description. From the little he'd known of her before he left the department, she'd lived up to her reputation. He knew from experience she could be tough, relentless and prickly to the point of standoffish.

Even now, he couldn't say she was overly approachable. That she had allowed him to invade her personal space was probably a big concession for her. And possibly a mistake. If she hoped to keep her job, she wasn't doing herself any favors by associating with the likes of him. But he suspected her version of doing the right thing might differ considerably from the department's. She came across as an independent thinker, and he liked that about her. He liked a lot of things about her, and that revelation had come as a surprise, considering his previous opinion.

She looked pensive, as if assessing how much she wanted to tell him. "This stays between us?"

"Goes without saying."

She nodded, but still seemed uneasy. "I think he could be working for Richard Mathison. If I'm right, he moved into the house next door to keep tabs on me." She glanced up to gauge his reaction. "See? Paranoid."

Trent moved over beside her and picked up the binoculars. He lifted them to his eyes and adjusted the focus ring as he peered out the window. "Who's keeping tabs on who?"

She grabbed the strap and pulled the binoculars from his hand. "Don't judge. I could be a bird-watcher for all you know."

He couldn't imagine anyone who struck him less like a bird-watcher. Not that there was anything wrong with the pastime. He was a big nature lover himself. But that was all beside the point...

"A notion like that doesn't just pop into your head out of the blue," he said. "What makes you think he's working for Richard Mathison?"

Her voiced hardened. "Because Gabriel Mathison threatened me, that's why. He said I had no idea how far his father would go to protect his precious reputation. His words. He implied that the injuries I sustained in the car accident are nothing compared to what's coming."

Trent scowled. "When did this happen?"

"He came to me see me last night in the hospital. I woke up, and there he was at the foot of my bed watching me sleep." She gave an exaggerated shudder. "Talk about creepy. I thought I was having a nightmare at first."

"What did you do?"

"Nothing I could do. He'd placed both my phone and the call button out of reach while I slept. I could have screamed, I suppose, but a part of me wanted to hear what he had to say. And I didn't want to give him the satisfaction of knowing he'd frightened me."

Tough as nails. "You don't think the threat was a bluff?"

"Do you? I mean, you heard the press conference. Richard Mathison is coming after me with a vengeance. He doesn't just want me fired. You said it yourself. He wants to make an example of me."

"But that doesn't explain why you think your new neighbor is involved."

"Because he *is* my new neighbor."

He gazed down at her in puzzlement. "There has to be more to it than that."

She tucked stray strands of hair behind her ears and sighed. "Like I said, I really didn't want to get into all this right now, but here goes. When I got home from the hospital earlier, he came through the hedge and struck up a conversation. He said he heard the car and thought it might be my landlord, but in hindsight, I think he was waiting for me."

"How would he know you'd been released from the hospital?"

"The same way one of my witnesses got relocated and another recanted her statement. Richard Mathison's reach is long and powerful."

"I've known that for a long time," he agreed. "Did Shaw say anything specific to trigger your suspicion?"

"It was a lot of little things. For instance, he told me that he'd leased the house next door for the summer, but he didn't even know the owner's name."

"Mrs. Dorman?"

"See? Even you remember. He said she'd gone to Florida to take care of her sister, but now I'm wondering if she even has a sister."

"That should be easy enough to find out," Trent said. "I'll make a few calls."

She was instantly defensive. "You don't have to go to all that trouble just to humor me. Besides, I'm perfectly capable of checking things out for myself. At least…I was."

"Let me guess. You've already been reprovisioned."

She looked up in alarm. "How did you know?"

"Standard operating procedure. Your passwords were

probably reset the minute you surrendered your badge and weapon. That's fine. Plenty of ways around a lockout. I'll let you know what I find out."

She looked as if she wanted to argue, then backed off with a nod. "Thanks. If it helps, he has history with the house. He said he lived there for a short time as a kid. He claims Martin Swann was like a surrogate uncle to him."

"Who's Martin Swann?"

"My landlord. He called him Uncle Marty." She wrapped the leather cord around the binoculars and set them aside. "Maybe it was just my imagination—or my paranoia—but when I saw them together earlier, I sensed a weird vibe between them. Like maybe Martin wasn't so happy to see him."

"Maybe we need to check out Uncle Marty, too," Trent suggested.

"He's lived in Seaside for a long time. He once told me that he's owned this property for over thirty years."

Trent glanced over his shoulder, taking in the small living area and compact kitchen. "Has he always rented out this space?"

"Just since his wife died, I think. Brandon mentioned that Martin used the apartment as a retreat whenever his wife had guests. Apparently, she was a lot more social than he was. Or is. He seems to be pretty much a hermit these days, but I'm not one to talk. I don't exactly have a bunch of friends knocking down my door to see how I'm doing."

He smiled. "I'm here."

"Yes, but you're not a friend. Not really. Not yet." She gave him a questioning look. "I'm not exactly sure what we are. Partners? Associates? Coconspirators?"

"How about a pair of shunned detectives working toward a common goal? A pair of misfits who have more in common than either of us would have ever thought twenty-four hours ago."

She gave a little laugh. "I guess that's true. And it doesn't even sound so bad when you put it that way."

He was relieved that she took his assessment in the light-hearted spirit in which he'd intended. Her smile was brief but warm. Almost electric. In the split second before she glanced away, something unexpected flashed between them. Not attraction, though Trent found himself drawn to her despite his past perceptions and her current reservations. Not *only* attraction, he amended, but a unique connection that only two people who had each walked an ill-fated path could experience.

"Trent? Did you hear what I said?" She scowled up at him. "You looked like you were a million miles away just now. Where did you go all of a sudden?"

"Nowhere. Just thinking. Anything else you remember about your conversation with Brandon Shaw?"

"It wasn't a lengthy discussion," she said. "But there is one more odd thing that happened. Someone brought two dozen white roses to my hospital room last night while I was asleep. Gabriel Mathison made a point of telling me about the message on the card. He had it memorized. At first, I thought he just wanted me to know how long he'd been in my room before I woke up. Now I think his intent was more sinister."

"What did the card say?"

"*See you soon, Sydney.* No name, no address, nothing else. Gabriel whispered that same message in my ear before he left my room. Then earlier, Brandon Shaw said the same thing to me at the bottom of the stairs. *See you soon, Sydney.* It's a common catchphrase. I know that. But the timing just seems—I don't know—too coincidental."

"I'm not big on coincidences," Trent said. "But let's play this out for a minute. If the Mathisons did plant him next door, you have to wonder about their endgame. What do they hope to gain by their continued harassment?"

"Just plain old revenge," Sydney said. "These are not good people."

"Agreed, but you've been taken off the case and suspended from the department. The prudent move would be to back off and keep a low profile before another witness decides to come forward. My guess is, you've got them spooked. Is it possible you stumbled across something incriminating that you don't even realize yet? The fact that Gabriel came to your hospital room in the middle of the night smacks of desperation."

"Or cockiness."

"I don't think either of them are as confident as they'd have us believe." A peal of laughter drew Trent's attention back to the window. He stared down into the backyard of the house next door, where two young women in bikinis had suddenly appeared in the water. "Looks like the pool party has turned out to be an intimate affair."

Sydney craned her neck. "I don't see Brandon."

"Maybe he's tending the grill."

She struggled out of the chair, and they stood side by side at the window watching the women giggle and shriek as they tried to mount air floats. "Something just occurred to me," Sydney mused. "He brought up a delivery for me earlier. Brandon, I mean. Maybe we could lift his prints from the cardboard box."

"Packages from a major carrier pass through dozens of hands before they get left at a front door. Lifting a clear set of prints might be difficult. But we can give it a go. Do you have a kit?"

"Not here. Do you?"

"Not on me. I'll bring one by tomorrow."

They returned their attention to the window. After a few minutes, Brandon came out of the house and sat down on the edge of the pool, kicking water toward the young women, who squealed and tried to paddle away. He jumped in after them and grabbed the nearest raft, dunking the occupant. She tried to surface, but he was on her in a flash, holding her under water until her companion came to her rescue by pounding on his back and tugging at his arms.

Trent muttered, "What the hell...?"

The woman came up sputtering and cursing and setting off another shrill yelp from her friend. They both climbed back on the air mattresses and paddled away as Brandon hitched himself out of the pool. Legs dangling, he leaned back on his elbows and lifted his gaze to Sydney's window, as if he knew they were there. As if he was amused rather than embarrassed that they'd witnessed the disturbing horseplay.

Sydney grabbed Trent's arm and tried to pull him away from the window. She lost her balance and would have tumbled to the floor if he hadn't caught her.

"You okay?"

Something that might have been surprise glinted in her eyes. Had she felt it, too? That little spark of awareness upon contact?

She swallowed. "Do you think he saw us?"

"Probably, but there's a glare on the window. He couldn't have seen much more than shadows." Trent glossed over the awkwardness of their interaction as he dropped his hands from her arms and reached for her crutches.

She gave a little hop to regain her balance. "I think that's being optimistic."

"Does it matter? His guests are making a lot of noise over there. It's only natural we'd get curious."

"Yes, but I don't want him to think I'm spying on him."

"Probably best not to let him see the binoculars, then."

She cut him a glance. "I'm serious. We shouldn't have been standing at the window like that. I know better. I was taught how to surveil by the best in the business."

Trent sobered. "I know you know what you're doing, but it bears repeating. Be careful with that guy. What we just witnessed was more than innocent roughhousing. He crossed a line."

To Trent's surprise, she accepted his warning without challenge. She may even have been grateful for his concern. "I'll be on guard," she promised. "Should we get back to our other business?"

Tempting, but he could see the weariness in her eyes. She was about done in, though she wouldn't likely admit it. "I think we've talked enough for one day. I'll call you tomorrow. We can pick back up when we're both fresh."

She walked him out to the porch. "I'm glad you came over. Everything you told me about those murders…it's a lot to take in. Fascinating but a bit overwhelming. I can see how you got caught up after the first interview."

He nodded. "It's hard to believe how under the radar they've remained."

She grew reflective. "What did you mean earlier when you said chronology is everything?"

"Remember yesterday when I told you the FBI eventually concluded the killer was clever enough to evade capture by varying his MO? I have a different theory. He was clever, but he was also evolving. I'll explain more tomorrow. I did warn you it's complicated."

"And getting more so all the time," she murmured.

"That's why I appreciate having another perspective. I can sometimes get lost in the weeds when I'm working alone."

She shrugged off his gratitude. "You know what they say. Two disgraced cops are better than one."

He grinned and started down the steps, turning to glance over his shoulder when she called his name.

She stared down at him, her expression solemn. "Be careful. Dealing with the Mathisons is one thing, but this strange little game you're playing with a serial killer is next level."

Chapter Five

After Trent left, Sydney put away the food and wiped the table. Normally, she would have taken the trash to the outside bin, but her first trip down the steps would have to wait until she felt less wobbly on crutches. She could always ask for help, of course, but that went against her nature. She'd always been independent. A broken ankle might slow her down, but she didn't intend to remain helpless or housebound for the full six weeks of her recovery.

Tonight, however, solitary confinement didn't seem so bad. The mundane task of tidying up had sapped her strength. She was glad that Trent had come over, but she was also relieved to be alone. She had a lot of thinking to do.

Lowering herself onto the recliner, she adjusted the blinds so that she could see out, but anyone looking up at the window wouldn't be able to see her. Then she opened her laptop and clicked on the links to Trent's podcast. The interview with the HPD detective popped up on her screen as a video. She hit Play with the intent of watching for only a few minutes to get a taste, but the material was so compelling she soon lost track of time.

When she finally finished the nearly two-hour interview, the sun had dipped beneath the treetops. At some point, the party next door had broken up or moved inside. The deserted air mattresses looked forlorn and slightly deflated, drifting on the surface of the pool. One of the women had left a pair of white sandals on the deck. Sydney fixated on the high-heel slides for a moment as she thought about all those missing left shoes. All those young lives cut short because of a predator's lust for taking them. What if Trent's hunch proved right? What if that same killer had returned with an even more voracious appetite?

The light faded rapidly with the setting sun. Dusk rolled in on a mild breeze. Sydney would have expected lights to come on in the house next door, but the windows remained dark as the garden grew shadowy. Where had everyone gone? She hadn't heard a car engine, and it was too far to walk to the nearest bars and restaurants. And those shoes remained poolside.

If Brandon and his guests hadn't left the property, what were they doing inside that dark house?

She wanted to believe her suspicions about him were unfounded. Maybe she really was prone to paranoia. Maybe she needed to take a step back and reevaluate, not only her priorities but also her motivation. But putting aside his timely appearance next door, something about him continued to niggle her. The horseplay in the pool earlier only reiterated her qualms about her new neighbor. There was more to Brandon Shaw than met the eye.

She watched the property for another few minutes before diving into Trent's second interview.

Doug Carter's story had been fascinating, but Eileen Ballard's account of the last moments she'd spent with her sister held Sydney enthralled. The woman's twenty-year crusade for justice had honed her storytelling skills. Sydney found herself holding her breath in places and gasping aloud in others. She started out taking notes but soon gave up and just listened intently.

Surprisingly, Trent was an unobtrusive host. Once again Sydney marveled at how vastly different her impression of him had been from the reality. She couldn't help but admire a man who had hit rock bottom but had somehow found the necessary desire and grit to reinvent himself. If she could get past her bruised pride and innate stubbornness, she just might learn a thing or two from him.

What to make of that smile they'd shared? That brief, knowing glance? It had been a while since she'd experienced the thrill of attraction brought on by a mere glance or touch. She'd concentrated on her career to the near exclusion of a social life. She told herself she didn't miss the complications of a relationship. She was in so much trouble at work, the last thing she wanted or needed was a romantic entanglement no matter how fleeting.

Keep right on telling yourself that. Keep reminding yourself that twenty-four hours ago, you wouldn't have given Trent Gannon the time of day.

But things changed. Sometimes in the blink of an eye, it seemed.

She couldn't help but wonder about his past, about the heroic woman he'd mentioned with such deep sorrow and regret. Maybe she'd ask the lieutenant about Trent's past the next time she saw him, although that might be a bit tricky, considering his contentious departure from the department.

Her place turned gloomy with only the computer screen for illumination. When the second episode finally concluded, she felt simultaneously exhausted and agitated. She put aside the laptop and sat in the dark, rehashing key points of the discussion. She heard a door open and close next door. She sat up straighter and lifted a blind with her fingertip so that she had a clearer view of the backyard.

A shadow slipped across the dark yard toward the side door of the garage. She heard the metallic rattle of the garbage cans and thought her neighbor might be taking the trash to the curb. Instead, he made several trips back and forth from the house to the garage. The overhead door rumbled as it lifted. A few minutes later, Brandon Shaw's car slowly backed down the driveway. Sydney couldn't make out any passengers, and she hadn't seen his guests exit the house. Maybe the women had parked their car down the street and had left through the front door.

Or…

Don't go there. Overreach is what got you in trouble in the first place.

Out on the street, the headlights arced as the vehicle turned east and then south at the intersection. She wondered how long he'd be gone. Now would be the perfect time to search his place—except for the fact that she could barely get around in her own apartment, let alone navigate an unfamiliar layout in the dark. And that was beside the dual obstacles of her steep stairs and his locked doors.

Bad idea. Tempting but not at all wise and went against everything her dad had taught her.

She watched until the taillights disappeared, and then she glanced at the clock on her phone. Barely ten o'clock. Still early by her pre-accident standards.

The podcast had left her restless and moody. She needed to talk to someone about what she'd just heard and about all the disturbing images floating around in her head.

She tapped Trent's number in the Recent Calls on her phone, then immediately had second thoughts. Too late. He answered on the first ring.

She tried to sound casual. "Hey, it's Sydney."

"Hey. Everything okay?"

Already his voice had become familiar to her and, in a way, comforting. Maybe because he was her only ally at the moment. "Everything is fine. Am I calling too late?"

"No, I'm up."

His slight hesitation only intensified her trepidation. What if he really had been asleep? Or worse, what if he had company? She knew next to nothing about his personal life except what he'd revealed earlier. Three years was a long time. He could have a serious girlfriend for all she knew. Or a wife. The absence of a wedding ring meant nothing. "Are you sure I'm not interrupting anything? We can talk tomorrow."

"I'm sitting here alone on my patio enjoying the evening breeze. So, no. You aren't interrupting anything."

She realized she'd been gripping the phone. She relaxed her fingers. "Are you waiting for the boat?"

"It's still a little early, but I'm keeping an eye out."

She took another breath. "Are you armed?"

There was a slight hesitation before he said, "Let's just say, I'm prepared."

She didn't know what that meant but sincerely hoped he knew what he was doing. "I'm glad you're taking precautions. This is no time to let down your guard. From what you told me earlier, he could already be nearby, watching your place. He could be observing you at this very moment, and you wouldn't even know it."

"That might be a good thing."

His response astounded her. "How could that be a good thing?"

"Any deviation from his pattern makes him vulnerable.

He's already taking risks. Getting bolder. Eventually, he'll make a mistake, and that's how we'll catch him."

"By using yourself as bait?"

"By luring him out into the open."

"You make it sound so easy," she said.

He gave a low chuckle. "That sounds easy to you?"

She wasn't amused. "You know what I mean. You're downplaying the danger. It's one thing to put yourself on the line, but he's not just watching your place, is he? How could he know about that little girl and her cat unless he's been watching your neighbor's house, too?"

"I know." His tone turned serious. "If it puts your mind at ease, the child and her mother left for Phoenix early this morning."

"Because of what happened?"

"No, the trip was already planned. They won't be back for several weeks. Plenty of time for us to do what needs to be done."

"I don't like this," Sydney said. "You're putting yourself in harm's way without any backup. And what about your neighbor? Shouldn't you warn him about the possibility of a killer lurking in the area?"

"I've briefed him. He's former military. Special Forces would be my guess, because he won't talk about his time in the service. Again, if it makes you feel any better, he's built like a tank and armed to the teeth. I couldn't ask for better backup."

"That's a relief, I guess." She glanced down into the shadowy yard next door. The moon was up, but the night seemed darker than usual and eerily silent. No passing cars. No barking dogs. She had the sudden and disquieting notion that someone could be watching her at that very moment.

She imagined a human shadow down by the oleanders. The silhouette vanished as she peered into the darkness.

"This whole discussion seems surreal," she said with a shiver. "Yesterday, my only concern was stopping Gabriel Mathison from leaving the country. Now I've been suspended from a job I love, and I'm working off the books helping a man I barely know to track a serial killer."

"Interesting turn of events, isn't it?"

"Interesting? That's one word for it." She tried to imagine him sitting in the dark, eyes peeled on the water in anticipation. Alert yet restless and edgy. But maybe that was another projection. He seemed pretty calm at the moment. More deliberate and self-possessed than he had a right to be under the circumstances. She was the one with jitters.

"You haven't told me why you called," he said. "Are you sure everything is okay over there? No more run-ins with Brandon Shaw?"

"He's not home. He left a little while ago. But he's not why I called." She put the phone on speaker as she tried to recapture her train of thought. "I just finished the interview with Eileen Ballard. It got me to thinking about the scarf you found and all the implications of that bloodstain. If there's even a slight chance that you're in possession of the killer's DNA, or the victim's, you have to go to the police."

"I came to you. You are the police."

She winced. "Probably not for long. And at the moment, my options are limited, as you've pointed out. There isn't much I can do to help besides offer an ear and moral support. Still, I have to say this again. You can't sit on evidence that important."

"Think about what you're advising me to do." His voice was a low rumble in her ear. Steady yet enigmatic. "What do you think will happen if I waltz into the station and claim the scarf I found tied around a cat's neck belonged to a woman who was murdered twenty years ago? How do you think they'll respond?"

She cringed. "Ugh. When you put it that way…"

"Exactly. It sounds ridiculous even to me, and I'm the one who found the damn thing. I don't have all that much credibility with the Seaside Police Department to begin with. How long do you think it would take for rumors to start swirling about my mental health? Or that I'm drinking again?"

She couldn't dispute his reasoning. "What if I talk to Dan Bertram?"

Something shifted in his voice. "I'd rather you didn't."

"Why not?"

"Let's just say, I don't hold him in the same regard as you and leave it at that."

She bristled at the implication. "Come on. You can't drop an innuendo like that and expect me to let it go without an explanation. I've known the man my whole life. Since my dad died, he's been more of a parent to me than my own mother. I deserve to know what you mean."

"I shouldn't have said anything."

"But you did."

He hesitated as if he really didn't want to get into it but recognized the very real possibility that she wouldn't let it go until he did. "Before you trust him to have your back, look into his connections to Richard Mathison."

She suppressed a gasp. "What connections? What are you talking about?"

"All I know is that I witnessed firsthand what you and I discussed earlier. You were right when you said Richard Mathison's reach is long and powerful. And I was right when I told you he has people in the police department who owe him favors."

"Dan Bertram isn't one of them," she insisted. "You're mistaken about him."

"Maybe I am. I hope so. But for now, neither of us should count on any help from that quarter. It's just you and me. That is, if you're still willing."

She took offense at the suggestion. "Do you think I'm so fickle or thin-skinned that I'd back out over one disagreement? Give me a little more credit than that."

"To be honest, you strike me as the opposite of fickle and thin-skinned."

She supposed that was meant as a compliment. "I won't say anything to the lieutenant. He probably wouldn't believe me anyway. He might even think I'm trying to divert attention from my own situation. A discredited cop crying wolf." She closed her eyes as the bitterness of her current reality sank in. "It seems we're both in the same boat when it comes to credibility. But I still say the DNA evidence on that scarf is too important to sit on. What about taking it to Doug Carter? He must have friends in the Houston Police Department. Technically, the seventh murder is still their case."

"The problem with that is timing and urgency," Trent said. "Houston is one of the largest human trafficking hubs in the country. The crime lab is backed up anywhere from six months to two years. A twenty-year-old cold case wouldn't be considered a priority. They could take the scarf and back-burner a DNA test indefinitely."

She sighed in frustration. "Then what do you suggest we do?"

"Our best bet at the moment is an independent lab. I know someone who knows someone who owes me a favor.

I'll push for a rush. With any luck, we could have the results by the end of the week."

"And then what? I hate to point out the obvious, but unless you know someone who knows someone in the FBI, we won't have access to any of their databases."

"One thing at a time," Trent said. "It's doubtful we'd turn up a match anyway. Otherwise, he wouldn't have risked leaving that scarf. He knows his DNA isn't in the system."

"Or he knows the blood belongs to the victim. You said he wants someone to know he's back."

"That would leave little doubt," Trent agreed. "But as I said, first things first. We need to find out if the stain is human blood. Then we'll go from there."

She checked the time on her phone. "No sign of the boat yet?"

"Unless he breaks another pattern, he won't show until straight-up midnight."

"Brandon Shaw said he rented the house next door to be close to the marina," she murmured.

"What?"

"He said he wanted to do nothing but fish and swim this summer. Probably doesn't mean anything." Neither did the white sandals abandoned on his pool deck. "I'm not even sure why I brought it up."

Trent was silent for a moment. "He couldn't have been more than nine or ten at the time of the first murder."

"I know. He just…"

"He bears watching for other reasons," Trent said.

She glanced out her window, trailing her gaze along the oleanders where she had spotted a shadow earlier. All was quiet next door, the house still dark. Her gaze went back to those sandals, and a shiver traced up her spine for no good reason.

"You still there?" Trent asked.

"There's a full moon tonight. Is that a good thing or bad?"

"It's to our advantage. The illumination will enhance thermal imaging. I'll be able to see farther and more clearly. Maybe he'll get careless and I'll even catch a glimpse of his face."

"Do you think he'll make contact again tonight?"

"Another scarf tied around a cat's neck? He won't be able to repeat that trick. Larry is safe inside, snoozing on his favorite chair. He'll start yowling to go out as soon as he wakes up, but too bad. Tonight, he's an indoor kitty."

She found his concern for the cat rather touching. A day ago, she would have thought it out of character, but she was learning each time they spoke that Trent Gannon was full of surprises and not at all how she had imagined him.

On impulse, she said, "I found the key to the storage locker. We can go through my dad's things together if you're still interested."

"I'm definitely interested. Tomorrow good for you? I can swing by your place in the afternoon and pick you up."

"I'll be here. I don't know what you hope to find, but I guess it can't hurt to take a look."

He was so quiet she thought he might be distracted by the boat. Then he said, "Your dad never mentioned Doug Carter?"

"Not that I recall. Why?"

"They shared information on their investigations for years. Doug had a lot of respect for your dad."

She tensed. "Why am I sensing a *but*?"

"The last few times they spoke, Doug felt your dad was holding out on him."

Sydney was quick to refute. "He wouldn't do that. He was the most honest, by-the-book cop I've ever known. There's no way he would have withheld important information on a murder investigation."

"No one is suggesting he did," Trent said. "Evidence and fact go into the official casefile. A good detective will keep his hunches close to the vest if he feels the need to."

The exact opposite of what she'd done in the Gabriel Mathison case. If she'd been a little more discreet and circumspect, she might not be in her current situation. "So that's why you want to look through his notes. You're hoping to find something that never made it to the official record."

"You knew him better than anyone. What do you think?"

"I can tell you that he was a stickler for detail."

"That could be all we need."

Now she was the one who fell silent. "Can I ask you something? It may sound far-fetched, but do you think it's possible the suspect made contact with my dad like he has with you? I mean, think about it. Dad was the first one who identified a single perpetrator. He was the one who brought in the FBI. Seems logical if the killer wanted to communicate with the police, he would have reached out to the one cop who had begun to figure him out."

"Not out of the realm of possibility," Trent said. "It certainly has precedent. Go back to the BTK Killer, who left notes and packages all over town for the police. Or the Zodiac killer, who sent all those cryptic messages and cyphers to the media. The list goes on and on. Why? Did you remember something?"

"Nothing concrete. Just something he said to my mother once." She paused. *"Don't let her go outside alone until we catch the bastard."*

"I take it she was referring to you?" Trent didn't sound

convinced. "That's a pretty generic warning. He could have been talking about any criminal."

"I told you it would sound far-fetched."

He tried to soften his skepticism. "I'm the one who found a bloodstained scarf tied around a cat's neck, remember? Just because it sounds far-fetched doesn't mean it's not true."

"Thanks for that." She reclined in the chair and elevated her injured foot. "I don't know why that conversation suddenly came back to me. Who knows if it's even real? But in my mind, I can hear him as clear as day."

"You don't remember anything more specific?"

She thought about her mother's response. "Nothing relevant. His concern really doesn't make sense, because I would have been a little kid at the time of those murders. I didn't fit the victim profile. The killer went after young women. So why was he afraid for my safety unless…"

"He had reason to be."

"Maybe it was the tone of his voice or a look in his eyes," she said. "Or maybe I'm taking too much pain medication and my thinking is all muddled. I just can't help wondering if the killer knew about me. If he somehow used me to send a message to my dad like he did with your neighbor's granddaughter."

Trent's voice took on a note of caution. "Let's see what turns up in your dad's notes before we jump to conclusions. In the meantime, get some rest. I keep forgetting that you just survived a major car crash and you were released from the hospital only a few hours ago. Try and put everything we discussed out of your head for the night. The interviews, too. We can pick back up tomorrow."

But that proved easier said than done. Sydney sat staring out into the night for a long time after the call ended.

Trent was right. She needed to sleep, but her mind wouldn't settle. How much of her anxiety could be attributed to the mess she'd made at work or to a new medication, she didn't know. She wasn't herself. Pain and exhaustion had taken a toll. Made her think things that would never have occurred to her in a less stressful state.

But recognizing her current vulnerabilities did little to ease her mind. She couldn't let go of the notion that the killer had known about her when she was a child. And he'd been waiting all these years for her to grow up.

TRENT SET THE alarm on his phone while he waited for the boat. Not that he was in any danger of falling asleep before midnight. As the hour approached, he'd never felt more alert. Nothing out of the ordinary would escape his attention tonight, no matter how slight a movement or sound. If the killer decided to come ashore, he was armed and ready. But as prepared as he was, the vibration of the silenced alarm still startled him. He turned off the sound and lifted his binoculars.

There he was. Right on time.

Trent's every muscle tensed as he watched the ghostlike vessel glide across the dark water, pausing as it always did directly out from the bungalow. Maybe it was his imagination, but the boat seemed farther away tonight, as if the pilot had calculated the necessary distance from shore to maintain his anonymity when observed through a night-vision lens.

Trent rose and strode barefoot down the path to the water's edge. Not that a few extra feet would enhance his visibility, but he supposed it was a psychological thing. A hollow act of bravado. He stood in ankle-deep water and adjusted the focus ring. For several long minutes, nothing happened. The only motion he could detect was the gentle rise and fall of the hull.

Then, just like the night before, a figure appeared starboard. The person looked to be wearing something over his head, like a cap or a hood to disguise his features. Despite the distance, he kept his face turned away from the shoreline.

He moved about the deck, coming in and out of view before disappearing for several minutes inside the cabin. When he came back out, he carried what looked to be a trash bag in one hand. Moving up to the rail, he flung the bag into the water.

Trent's attention remained riveted. Judging by the size and the ease with which the bag had been tossed, he couldn't be disposing of a body. Not an intact body, at least. *Then what the hell was it?* He doubted someone would make a midnight journey out to the bay just to dump their everyday garbage.

The figure went back inside the cabin and returned a moment later with yet another bag, which he also hurled into the water. Then he stood peering over the rail until presumably the items sank. After a few minutes, he turned his head toward the shoreline. Toward Trent.

For a moment, Trent could have sworn they made eye contact. Strange, because the distance was so great that he couldn't see the man clearly despite the moonlight. He appeared little more than a grainy silhouette against a green field. And yet Trent experienced a flash of familiarity that turned his blood cold.

He watched until the boat disappeared into the darkness, and then he made his way slowly back to the patio. He tried to keep the man's silhouette fresh in his mind as he searched his memory banks for an image or a trigger that would give him a name or a face.

But in the next instant, he scoffed at the notion. The killer had been active when Trent was a kid. Sydney's theory about a connection through her dad was at least somewhat plausible. Trent had no reason to believe his path had ever crossed with the killer's. He wasn't thinking straight. The adrenaline rush that had sustained him throughout the previous night and most of the day faded as grim reality set in. He hadn't been a cop for nearly three years. Even before his dismissal, he'd never dealt with the ruthless cunning of a serial predator. What made him think he could match wits now?

Because you were once a good detective and sooner or later, even the cleverest of killers slip up. Because if you don't find him, who will?

Plopping down in the creaky lawn chair, he lifted the binoculars one last time to make certain the cruiser had vanished. The moonlit water looked deceptively calm. He thought about waking up his neighbor and asking for his boat key. With a little luck, he might be able to find whatever had been tossed overboard. But even knowing the approximate location, he'd still have to search a long stretch of ocean floor and his diving experience was limited at best. A night dive presented a whole new set of challenges.

Maybe Sydney was right. Maybe it was time to bring in the professionals, but he had a bad feeling about the outcome. Even if by some miracle he could get someone to take him seriously, a police presence might do nothing but drive the killer deeper underground. Besides, he'd made contact with Trent for a reason. What that reason was, he had no idea, but he intended to find out.

As the minutes ticked by, the waiting started to get to him. He told himself to go inside, lock the doors and keep watch from the window. Exhaustion bred carelessness. But he ignored his better instincts and remained outside until he was certain the boat had had time to come ashore.

He sat in the dark and listened for the sound of a car engine or stealthy footfalls slipping through the shadows. Earlier, Larry had been caterwauling to get out, but all was silent now except for the occasional tinkle of the wind chimes on the boathouse. An hour went by without incident. He relaxed and even caught himself nodding off. Told himself once again to go inside, get some sleep. He'd been running on fumes for the past twenty-four hours. He was starting to hear things. See things.

Slapping his cheeks to revive himself, he sat up straighter in the chair. He'd definitely sensed something out of the ordinary.

The hair at his nape prickled. Not his imagination. He was no longer alone.

His gun lay on the ground beside his chair. Sliding his hand between the seat and the armrest, he closed his fingers around the handle and brought the weapon to his side as he slowly rose.

The wind chimes had gone silent. He could hear no sound at all except for the gentle ripple along the shoreline. Yet his every instinct told him the killer was somewhere in the dark, watching and waiting.

Trent moved from the moonlit patio into the yard where he took cover in the landscaping. He crouched behind a palmetto, his senses on high alert as he slowly scanned his surroundings. Nothing. All was quiet.

He was beginning to think he had imagined a presence when something brushed against his leg. He looked down into Larry's upturned face. Then he knelt and ran his hand along the cat's backbone. "How the hell did you get out?" he whispered.

Turning back to the bungalow, he scanned the porch and then trailed his gaze over every darkened window. Had the killer been inside his house? Was he there now, hiding under a bed or at the back of a closet until Trent was asleep and at his most vulnerable?

He couldn't have gained entry through the unlocked back door without Trent seeing him from the patio. The front door was dead-bolted. A forced entry through a window would surely have attracted his attention.

Staying low, he circled the premises, looking for an entry point. When he didn't find anything suspicious, he returned to the back of the house and eased up the steps onto the porch, then through the tiny mudroom into the kitchen. He knew every inch of the bungalow. The shadowy shapes of his furniture. The creaking floorboards in the hallway. Even the smell of it. When weather permitted, he kept his windows open to keep the musty scent at bay. Living so close to the water in an old house, mold and mildew were constant callers. Tonight, he could detect another scent, foreign and so elusive as to be nothing more than his imagination.

He moved quickly from room to room, scanning all the hiding places, and then he went back through for a more thorough search. His senses still on alert, he paused in the hallway outside his office as an unexpected draft skimmed along his bare arms. His office was on the opposite side of the house from the patio, making it a likely entry point. But he hadn't noticed an open window in his initial reconnaissance of the perimeter. Which meant someone had possibly gone out the window after Trent had entered the house.

He remained motionless, listening for the slightest sound that would signal an intruder's whereabouts. Then he sidled up to the door, checking the corners in one sweeping glance before stepping inside. Weapon in his right hand steadied with his left, he searched the room and adjoining closet. He was certain every window in the house had been closed and locked earlier, but the wooden frames were weathered and splintered in places and the latches rusted. It wouldn't take much muscle or skill to pry open a catch.

He stood sideways to the window so that he could search the site without turning his back to the hallway. The only movement he could detect was the flutter of leaves in the breeze. If someone had been inside the house, they were gone now. To be on the safe side, Trent shut and locked the window before once again combing the premises.

This time he turned on lights as he checked every room. When he found nothing else amiss, he went back to his office. He didn't know what he expected to find. Another article of bloodstained clothing or a left shoe perhaps.

It took him several minutes to realize that the whiteboard had been subtly altered.

SYDNEY WAS SO tired by the time she finally turned in that she made quick work of brushing her teeth and washing her face. Instead of undressing, she merely kicked off her shoes and collapsed on top of the covers in her sweatpants and tank top, her crutches within easy reach in case she needed to get up during the night.

She felt certain she'd fall asleep instantly, she was that exhausted, but the moment her head hit the pillow, the pain in her ankle intensified. She tried propping her foot up, but the elevation put even more pressure on her bruised rib so that every breath she took was pure agony. To make matters worse, she couldn't even toss and turn in the hopes of finding a more comfortable position. She could do nothing but lie on her back and stare up at the ceiling in abject misery.

When she could stand it no longer, she reached for a pain pill and washed it down with water from the bottle on her nightstand. She wanted to heed Trent's advice to go easy on the medication, but enough was enough. She needed to sleep. Tomorrow she would start tapering off. The pain would be easier to tolerate when she had something to occupy her mind with. Right now, all she could think about was the pulsing ache inside the hot, itchy cast.

When the throbbing finally eased and she was able to doze off, she slept deeply.

Sometime later she was startled awake by a noise. She fought her way up through a thick curtain of cobwebs, certain that someone had been banging on her door. But already the sound had faded, and she realized she must have been dreaming. No one would come beating on her door at this hour. No one with innocent intent.

Pushing herself back against the headboard, she picked up the phone to check the time. Just after two. She'd only been asleep for an hour or so. She'd stayed up late listening to podcasts in case Trent decided to call and let her know about the boat. The phone had remained annoyingly silent. She could have called him, of course, but she thought it best not to distract him. If he really intended to use himself as bait, he needed to be fully alert.

The pain in her ankle had subsided, but the reprieve hadn't come without a cost. She felt groggy and disoriented. Unsettled.

She would definitely ease off the pain medication. Trent wasn't the only one who needed to remain alert. From now on, she'd rely on willpower and an over-the-counter painkiller if she grew desperate enough—

Another sound intruded. She wasn't dreaming this time. She was cognizant enough to distinguish the difference.

The noise came again. Not a sharp knock or rap, but a thump, muted and distant. Normally, she wasn't the type to overreact to an unidentified sound in the middle of the night. She knew how to take care of herself. But her injuries made her vulnerable and more cautious.

Swinging her legs over the side of the bed, she grabbed her crutches. Maneuvering through the dark apartment, she paused at the front window to glance out at the narrow porch and landing area. She couldn't see anyone outside her door or at the bottom of the stairs. Whatever noise she'd heard had ceased once she got up.

She put her eye to the peephole. Still nothing.

"Who's there?" she called from behind her locked door. "I'm armed," she warned.

Silence.

She moved back to the window and searched for a moment longer before she opened the door and stepped out on the porch. The moon was still up but now partially shrouded by clouds that had rolled in from the gulf. She could smell rain in the breeze that ruffled the leaves and intensified the perfume from her landlord's garden. His place was dark, as were all the other houses up and down the street. The whole neighborhood seemed preternaturally silent. Shivering, she swept her gaze over the yard and into the shadows.

If someone had climbed the steps moments earlier to knock on her front door, the person had departed as soon as they realized she was up. She discarded the idea of an intruder. She hadn't heard footfalls on the steps. It was hard to descend a creaky wooden staircase without making a sound.

Another notion niggled. What if they hadn't gone down the steps? The landing extended a few feet around the corner of the apartment. Someone could be crouched against the wall, waiting for her to go back inside. Or waiting to spring out of the darkness and push her down the stairs.

Instinctively, she moved back into the doorway, shielding herself in the deep shadows. She told herself to play it safe. A serial killer resurrected from her dad's past might well be on the prowl. *Go back inside, lock the door and grab a weapon.* Instead, she waited. When no sound came to her, she eased along the wall until she could peer around the corner. No one was there.

She let out a quick breath of relief. The sound must have been a tree limb brushing against the side of the building or across the roof. Or the bump of a loose shutter somewhere nearby. The sound had filtered into her dream and manifested the knock on her door.

As she turned to go inside, a movement in the yard next door checked her. She pressed back into the shadows as Brandon Shaw came around the corner of his garage. He gazed across the backyard for a moment before he strode around the pool and picked up the abandoned sandals. Returning to the garage, he lifted the lid on the trash can and dropped the shoes inside.

He made another pass around the pool and garden area, his attention focused on the ground as if he were searching for something. After a few minutes, he disappeared through the back door of the house. No lights came on. Maybe he'd gone straight to bed. It was very late. Was he just now returning from wherever he'd gone to earlier? Sydney hadn't heard a car engine, but she'd been asleep until the phantom sound at her door had awakened her.

She eased back around the corner of the building only to pause yet again as something below caught her eye. She remained frozen as her eyes adjusted to the darkness and a silhouette took shape.

Martin Swann seemed oblivious to her presence as he hunkered in the oleanders, his gaze fixed on the house next door.

Chapter Six

"I haven't been able to find out much about your next-door neighbor," Trent told Sydney the following day as he sat across from her at her dining table. It was early afternoon, and he'd brought over enough barbeque to feed an army. Neither of them stood on ceremony. They removed the plastic lids from the containers and dug in. Potato salad, baked beans, brisket. Sydney happily filled her plate. Her appetite had returned with a vengeance, and she resolved to getting back to the gym sooner rather than later.

"I should clarify," Trent said, "I haven't been able to find anything yet. But I will. If this guy has skeletons, I'll dig them up."

"*We'll* dig them up," she clarified. "Just because I'm suspended doesn't mean I'm completely without means. I do have resources outside the police department." She picked up her fork. "Thank you for bringing this over, by the way. I haven't had a meal like this in ages."

He played down the gesture. "The restaurant was on the way and we both have to eat."

"Reminds me of when I was a kid and Dad would bring barbecue home from this little hole-in-the-wall joint on Market Street. We'd eat on the deck, just the two of us, and

I'd tell him about my day. Those conversations must have been boring to him, but he never let on."

"What about your mom?"

Sydney waited a beat, then tried to say matter-of-factly, "She left when I was thirteen."

"I'm sorry. I didn't mean to pry."

"No, it's okay." She shrugged. "I came to terms with her indifference a long time ago. Or at least, I pretend that I have. She'd be the first to admit that she was never cut out to be a wife and mother. Especially a mother. She didn't have the patience or the desire to deal with a difficult child."

He lifted a brow. "You were difficult?"

"Difficult by her standards. Meaning I didn't sit in my room and read all day. I liked to wander. Which, come to think of it, probably also suited her fine so long as I stayed out of her hair. My dad was the one who worried. He'd come out looking for me if I wasn't home by dark. Probably had something to do with the kind of people he dealt with all day."

"No doubt. Do you still see your mom?"

"Not very often. She lives in Austin with her artist boyfriend. I've driven up a couple of times for a visit. It was awkward. We don't have much in common. I think we're better off in a long-distance relationship. Anyway…" She poured warm barbecue sauce over her brisket. "What about you? Does your family live around here?"

"My parents were killed in a car wreck when I was in college. I lost my sister three years ago…" He paused. "It's just me now."

"I'm so sorry." Sydney didn't know what else to say. Then something occurred to her. "You were talking about your sister yesterday. You said she was the most heroic person you ever knew."

He nodded. "She was a lot younger than me. Just a kid when our parents died. I moved back home after the accident. Technically, I raised her, but she took care of me, too. She got sick her freshman year of college. A rare kind of bone cancer. She endured one treatment after another until…" He trailed off again. "We spent a lot of time in the hospital."

Sydney reached over and touched his hand briefly. "I can't imagine how hard that must have been."

"It's been a few years. I've had time to make peace."

In the face of his loss and suffering, she felt petty for her estrangement with her mother. *Maybe I'll call her when this is all over.*

"Things got a little deep there." His smile was still strained. "It wasn't my intent to unload on you like that. You've had a pretty rough go of it yourself." He seemed to shake off his dark mood as he pointedly observed her full plate. "But I'm glad to see you're feeling better."

She appreciated his effort and responded in kind. "Should I be embarrassed?"

"For being hungry? Not in my book. Nothing wrong with having a healthy appetite. Like I said, you'll need all your strength for getting around on those crutches. Speaking of…seems like your mobility has improved since yesterday. You've been practicing."

"You might not think so if you'd seen me stumble on the way to the door," she told him. "But maybe we should get back to Brandon Shaw. I didn't expect you to get started on a background check so soon. You have a lot more important things on your mind at the moment. Like using yourself as bait to lure a serial killer out of hiding…and keeping yourself alive in the process."

"No reason I can't do all of the above," he said between bites.

Her fork paused in midair as she stared across the table at him. "You're so nonchalant about this whole thing. I worry you're not taking the necessary precautions."

"Believe me, I am."

"So, what happened last night? Did the boat show up?"

"Yes, but we'll get into all that later. I'd rather focus on your neighbor right now."

Before she could press him about the boat, he said, "It's a little strange for someone his age to be so conspicuously absent from social media. No posts, tweets or images on any of the major platforms."

"He's not completely absent," she told him. "He teaches an online class in creative writing. I found his videos with a simple internet search."

"I saw those, too." Trent paused to swig his ice tea. "The videos look pretty damn polished. I know a little something about the editing process. It's a lot more time consuming than most people realize. Makes you wonder. If he's working for Richard Mathison, why go to all that trouble to create an elaborate cover? Why not just say he's on vacation since he's only supposed to be here for the summer?"

"I've thought about that. For one thing, it gives him an excuse for having video equipment. He could have a camera trained on my place twenty-four hours a day for all we know." She glanced toward the window and shuddered. "And for another, maybe he really is a down-and-out writer looking to make some extra cash. I would guess he's close to Gabriel Mathison's age. Maybe they knew each other at college, and he's done side jobs for the family for years. Or who knows? Maybe they met in a bar, and it's a strangers-on-a-train situation."

Trent looked amused. "That's thinking outside the box."

"I'm just saying. Every good cover has a hint of truth in

it. Brandon Shaw could be his pen name. Maybe that's why you haven't been able to locate his social media accounts."

He nodded his approval. "It's a leap, but I like where you're going with this. If he's using an alias, that would explain why I haven't been able to find him in any of the usual government databases. No tax, property or employment records. No arrests, tickets or warrants. Have you talked to your landlord? Maybe he knows the guy's real name."

"I haven't had a chance. But I'm glad you brought up Martin. I've got something to tell you about him, too."

"I'm all ears."

She blotted her lips on a paper napkin, marveling at the easy nature of their banter. Not only was she comfortable in Trent's company, she was also starting to look forward to his visits. He'd come over today ostensibly to pick her up so that they could search the storage unit for her dad's notebooks. When he showed up at her door with food, she could hardly turn him down. Not that she'd wanted to. As much as she valued her independence, she had to admit it was nice having someone look out for her for a change.

She was still amazed at how quickly her attitude had changed. Three years ago, she could never have imagined working with Trent Gannon in any capacity. Now she could hardly think of anything else. He'd offered her an interesting proposition when she badly needed a distraction, and he'd suggested an intriguing partnership when most of her colleagues had turned their backs on her. Already she was starting to think of him as a friend.

More than a friend, if she were honest, but it was best to keep things low-key while they got to know each other. She appreciated his honesty. It couldn't have been easy revisiting past tragedies and mistakes. Regardless of her new attitude, there was no need to rush into anything. She'd made that mistake before, and it hadn't ended well. She was a lot more careful these days. Besides, he might not even feel the same way, although she'd caught a lingering glance on more than one occasion when he thought her attention was diverted elsewhere. Like now, as he watched her intently from across the table.

He cocked his head. "Well? Don't leave me hanging."

"What?"

"You were going to tell me what you found out about Martin Swann."

She shook off her momentary reverie and forced her focus back to the matter at hand. "It's not so much what I found out. It's where I saw him. He was hiding in the bushes last night. Or early this morning, to be precise. Must have been around two."

His brows shot up. "That's not a euphemism, I take it. You literally saw him hiding in the bushes?"

She recounted the events of the previous evening while he ate.

"Did he see you?" Trent asked when she paused.

"I don't think so. His attention seemed laser-focused on the house next door."

"Why do you think he was spying on Shaw?"

"I have no idea. I told you yesterday I sensed a strange vibe between them. After last night, I'm really curious about their relationship. I have a feeling there's more to their back-story than Brandon wanted me to know."

Trent contemplated her revelation for a moment. "Maybe we should go downstairs and have a chat with Martin Swann."

"I don't know if that's a good idea. He likes to keep to himself. I'm not sure he'd even answer his door if he spotted you. Besides, I thought you were in a hurry to get to the storage unit."

"We've got all afternoon. That is, unless you're in a rush for some reason."

"No, but I think I should talk to Martin alone. He's used to having me around. I'll just casually work Brandon into the conversation without appearing to pry. Or without letting on that I saw him hiding in the bushes last night."

"That's one way to go about it," Trent said. "Or you could just ask him point-blank why he was spying on the neighbor. Catching him off guard might be illuminating."

"It might also put him on the defensive, and then I wouldn't find out anything."

"It's your call." Trent clicked the plastic lids onto the food containers and stood. "Are you done? Should I put the leftovers in the fridge so you'll have something to munch on later?"

"You don't have to wait on me." She scooted back her chair. "I'm doing okay. See?" Balancing on one foot, she stacked her dishes.

He continued to gather up the leftovers. "It doesn't make you weak to accept help, you know."

"Now you sound like Lieutenant Bertram."

He gave her an enigmatic look but didn't respond.

"You're never going to convince me he's a dirty cop," she said.

He looked as if he wanted to argue, then shrugged. "Just watch your back, okay? That's good advice, regardless."

"I'm not the one using myself as bait, but your point is taken."

He nodded and changed the subject. "You say Brandon Shaw left earlier in the evening with the two women we saw in the pool?" He picked up the leftovers and headed for the kitchen.

"I assumed so. I saw his car drive off just before I called

you. I didn't see another vehicle arrive or depart. But that's another odd thing." His question brought back the strange incident with the abandoned shoes, and she quickly filled him in.

Trent came back to the table. "You're right. That does sound a little odd. You'd think he'd have the courtesy of returning the shoes or at least hanging on to them until the owner could come back for them. But I can't say I'm surprised after what we witnessed in the pool yesterday. Holding a woman's head underwater until her friend has to come to her rescue isn't exactly gentlemanly behavior."

"I've had a bad feeling about him from the start," Sydney said.

"I know you have." Trent walked over to the window to stare down into the yard next door. "What's he been up to today?"

"I haven't seen him. Maybe he's sleeping in after a late night. Or maybe he's working on a new video." She hobbled over to the window. "He told me yesterday that he posts new videos on Tuesdays and hosts a live chat every Thursday evening so that his students and viewers can ask questions and participate in critiques. He made a point of inviting me to join in."

"What prompted that?"

"He seemed to think I'd get bored with too much time on my hands. He's not wrong about that," she said. "I didn't think much about the invitation at first. School was never my thing, so I more or less brushed him off. But in hindsight, I have to wonder why he even mentioned the classes to me in the first place."

"Maybe he was reinforcing his cover," Trent suggested.

"Or there's something he wants me to see or hear in those videos."

"Like what?"

She shook her head, deep in thought. "All I know for sure is that I'm now more inclined to take his bloody classes."

"Who knows? You may learn something," Trent teased. "Then you can write a book about our exploits."

Our exploits? "I can guarantee I won't be writing any books. I struggle to get through my incident reports. Paperwork is one thing I won't miss about being a cop, scorned or otherwise."

"I hear that."

She plopped down on the recliner and opened her laptop. "I want to show you something."

"About Shaw?"

"About his videos and what he may or may not want me to see. Maybe I'm reaching, but..." She scrolled through her bookmarked sites. Before she could tilt the laptop so that Trent had a view of the screen, he sat down on the side of the chair and threw an arm across the back. His nearness made her self-conscious. Made her heart beat a little faster so that she had to quickly remind herself the point of his visit.

"What are we looking for?" he asked.

"Like I said, I could be grasping at straws, but I found something curious about these videos. I checked the time stamp. Brandon Shaw uploaded the first one last Tuesday. I know it was shot next door because I recognize Mrs. Dorman's sunroom. See all those shelves behind the desk? That's where she displayed her rare houseplants and her favorite pottery. She was extremely proud of her collection. She said it took years to assemble, and some of the pieces had become quite valuable."

"You're using the past tense."

"What?" She turned to meet his gaze. He was so close

she could see the dark rim around his gray irises and a tiny freckle at the corner of his bottom lip. She swallowed. "Slip of the tongue, I guess."

He didn't look convinced. "You really think Brandon Shaw did something to her, don't you?"

"I know it sounds ridiculous. Maybe it's all the talk about a serial killer. I'm not usually this paranoid, but I actually thought about searching his house when I saw him drive off last night."

Trent looked alarmed. "That's a really bad idea."

"I know. My dad would turn over in his grave. Besides..." She lifted her injured foot. "I can't exactly run these days if I'm caught in the act."

"Running might not do you much good when he knows where you live." Trent's tone was light, but his expression had sobered. "Promise you won't do anything that risky unless I'm around to have your back."

"Says the man trying to single-handedly trap a serial killer."

"I don't have a broken ankle."

She sighed. "You don't have to keep reminding me. I'm painfully aware of my limitations."

"You say that now, but once boredom sets in, you may be tempted to mix things up. Being cooped up for too long makes people like us edgy."

"People like us?"

"We get bored, we get anxious, we get impulsive. Sometimes to the detriment of ourselves and those around us."

"You've got me all figured out, do you?"

Their gazes met again, and she found herself fixating on the freckle at the corner of his mouth. Why had she never noticed before the fullness of his bottom lip or the barest hint of a dimple in his chin? And why was she wondering now what kind of kisser he'd be? Did he employ finesse and technique, or was he more aggressive and impulsive, a real balls-to-the-wall type?

Apparently, she wasn't going to find out anytime soon. He continued their conversation without missing a beat. "At least give me a chance to look into Brandon Shaw's background before you take matters into your own hands."

She nodded and glanced back down at the laptop screen. Pausing the video, she went to a full-screen view. "Assuming he needed a day or two to shoot and edit the video before he uploaded, he's been in that house for at least a week. But I didn't meet him until yesterday. He led me to believe that he'd only moved in a few days ago."

"A week is a few days," Trent said.

"No, a week is several days, but the point is, he's been here longer that he let on, and he's removed all of Mrs. Dorman's things. Now, why would he do that? He only has a short-term lease. If she's coming back soon, why go to the trouble of getting rid of her plants and boxing up her pottery?"

"Isn't it possible Mrs. Dorman packed up her collection before she left? Maybe she didn't want to take a chance with anything breakable or valuable. She could have given the plants to a friend or neighbor to look after."

"Sounds perfectly plausible."

"But?"

"He's installed himself in an elderly woman's home and has removed her personal belongings. If that doesn't send up a red flag, I don't know what would."

"Talk to Martin Swann," Trent said. "Find out what he knows before we jump to any more conclusions."

The loud peal of her ringtone interrupted the discussion. She glanced at the screen before she picked up her phone. "It's Lieutenant Bertram."

"Go ahead and answer it."

She vacillated. "I don't think I want to hear what he has to say."

"Maybe it's good news." Trent rose. "Just answer the damn phone. I'll step outside and give you some privacy."

"You don't need to go. Just…" She held up a finger as she greeted the lieutenant and then listened for a moment before setting the phone aside.

"That was quick," Trent observed.

"Turns out I can't go to the storage unit with you, after all." She picked up the key from the side table and dropped in his hand. "You go without me. The lieutenant wants to see me at the station a-sap."

"Did he say why?"

"No, but he sounded tense." She worried her bottom lip. "That can't be good."

"Again, don't jump to conclusions," he advised. "And don't go in with an attitude. No matter what happens, try to keep your cool. Don't be goaded into losing your temper or saying something in the heat of the moment that might come back to bite you later."

She tried to muster a smile. "Voice of experience?"

"You know it. Do as I say, not as I've done."

"Things haven't turned out so badly for you."

His amusement faded. "I've made the best of a bad situation, but I'm not a cop and I never will be again. That's not the outcome I want for you."

Before she had time to prepare, his hand came up to feather along her cheek. His touch was gentle and so brief as to be an afterthought. The fleeting contact probably meant nothing at all, Sydney told herself. But her heart fluttered just the same.

Trent wanted to drop her at the station and wait outside for moral support, but she declined the offer. She needed a little distance. And if the meeting ended as she feared, she'd prefer to be alone on that long ride home. Besides, the lieutenant had insisted on sending a car for her. She wanted to take the gesture as a good sign, but given everything that had gone down in the past forty-eight hours, she'd be naive not to brace for the worst.

After Trent left, she spent a few minutes freshening up before tackling the outside staircase. She took his advice and scooted down the steps. Not a very dignified descent, but at least she made it to the bottom without incident. While she waited at the curb for her ride, she cast a doubtful glance at the sky. Clouds had moved in, and she could feel an occasional raindrop, but she wasn't about to go back up the stairs for an umbrella.

Next door, Brandon Shaw backed his vehicle out of the garage and reversed down the driveway. He seemed so preoccupied that he didn't even notice her at first. When he finally spotted her, he gave a brief wave before he turned the vehicle and accelerated toward the intersection.

Sydney wondered where he was going in such a hurry. She watched until his car disappeared around the corner, and then she turned to glance up his driveway. The oleanders obscured her view of the pool area, but she knew from memory that the trash can where he'd tossed the white sandals sat against the garage wall. Shifting her position, she wavered for a moment as she recalled Trent's warning about not doing anything reckless without backup. Surely a peek inside a trash can didn't constitute rash behavior. Besides, the lieutenant's car would arrive at any moment. She probably had five minutes at the most to explore.

She checked up and down the street and then over her

shoulder. None of her neighbors were out and about, including Martin Swann. Without the deterrent of prying eyes, she found it a little too easy to throw caution aside. With one final scan of her surroundings, she stepped through the oleanders into the neighboring yard. Now she was officially trespassing. She excused the transgression by reminding herself that sometimes it was necessary to be proactive.

Pausing yet again to reconnoiter, she swept her gaze over the house. The style was a seventies ranch with lots of windows and sliders. The blinds were up in the sunroom. She was tempted to crutch over and peer through the glass. It would be interesting to see if anything else had changed besides Mrs. Dorman's shelf décor. Given the time constraint, she had to content herself with searching the trash can.

Maneuvering up the driveway to the garage, she leaned a crutch against the wall to free one hand. The moment she lifted the lid, a foul odor emanated from the depths of the receptacle, triggering her gag reflex. Slamming the lid down, she waved aside a fly as she hopped back from the stench.

She was no stranger to the various odors of a crime scene. Her jurisdiction was close enough to Houston on one side and to the border on the other that drug- and human-trafficking-related homicides often trickled down into the smaller communities. Not to mention the occasional murder for hire and crime of passion. She knew what death smelled like. The reek rising from the trash can was more akin to rotting meat than human decomposition. That was some comfort, she supposed.

Covering her mouth and nose with her shirt, she tentatively lifted the lid and peered inside. The makeshift mask did little to smother the pungent smell. Swallowing back her revulsion, she used a stick to poke around in the garbage.

Food scraps, empty wine bottles, a few things in plastic bags that she couldn't identify. No white sandals. At least not lying on top of the refuse, as she would have expected. Maybe Brandon had had second thoughts and fished them out. Maybe he was returning them to their owner even now. Somehow, she doubted it.

She poked and prodded for another few minutes before replacing the lid and tossing aside the stick. Grabbing her crutch, she rounded the corner, intent on having a quick search of the pool area, but then she noticed that the side door of the garage stood open. That gave her pause.

It was one thing to go through someone's garbage, quite another to enter a neighbor's premises without invitation or a warrant or even probable cause. She was walking a very thin line. She could almost hear her father's stern admonition.

Don't do it, Syd. Don't you cross that line on nothing but a hunch.

Okay, but what if Brandon Shaw really did work for Richard Mathison? What if he was staying in the house in order to familiarize himself with her habits and weaknesses? Finding out what he was up to could give her an advantage or at least even the playing field.

Of course, she was going to check inside the garage. There had never really been any doubt. She'd come this far, and her suspicions regarding Brandon Shaw had only intensified since last night. She was more certain than ever that he wasn't the amiable neighbor he pretended to be.

Pushing the door wider, she swung inside on the crutches. The garage was dim despite windows on either side, and the space seemed cavernous without any vehicles. Mrs. Dorman parked her tiny Fiat beneath the attached carport on the other side of the house. She preferred to use the garage for storage. Despite all the gardening tools and equipment, the area was tidy and well organized, with plenty of space for a single vehicle. The smaller tools and equipment were tucked away in a cabinet or hanging from a wall or ceiling hook. Bags of potting soil and mulch were stacked against the wall while organic fertilizers and pesticides were stored on open shelving. The only thing that seemed out of place for an avid gardener was the enormous chest-style freezer that hummed at the back of the garage. Why would an elderly woman who lived alone need that much freezer space?

Just another oddity in a litany of inexplicable things, Sydney decided. Like the fact that Mrs. Dorman had been called away to tend to her sister at the same time Brandon Shaw had been looking for a short-term rental in the area. Like how he'd removed her houseplants and prized pottery pieces so quickly, as if he didn't expect her to return. Like how he had uttered the exact same catchphrase that had been written on the card that had accompanied the white roses from an anonymous admirer.

A refrigerator for keeping cold drinks handy would be understandable, especially for someone who spent so much time outdoors. But the size and shape of Mrs. Dorman's freezer reminded Sydney a little too much of a coffin. She started to imagine all sorts of dire possibilities. *You really think Brandon Shaw did something to her, don't you?*

By this time, she'd moved several feet into the garage. She glanced over her shoulder toward the open door. Coast was still clear. She inched farther into the shadowy interior, the rubber tips on her crutches thumping on the concrete floor. The stench from the trash can was still trapped in her nostrils when she paused in front of the freezer. Or was the smell only in her imagination?

She held her breath and reached for the latch, tested the lid and then lifted it gingerly. Condensation drifted from the opening. She hesitated to push the top all the way back, afraid of what she might find beneath the vapor—

"What do you think you're doing?"

Chapter Seven

Sydney's heart leaped into her throat. She thought at first Brandon Shaw had returned, and she braced herself for a confrontation even as she tried to come up with a plausible excuse for invading his private space. In the next instant, she recognized the voice and let out a breath of relief, though an encounter with her landlord would still be awkward under the circumstances. The only thing she had going for her was that "Uncle Marty" didn't belong here, either.

The freezer lid closed with a swoosh as she turned and said casually, "The same thing you are, I imagine. I'm looking for Brandon."

"In *there*?"

She couldn't tell if he was joking or not. Glancing back at the freezer, she said with a shrug, "Oh, that? No. I was just checking on something." She hurried to change the subject. "Have you seen him this morning?"

"He's not here. I heard his car leave a little while ago." Martin's expression never wavered. Was he suspicious? Annoyed? Curious? Sydney couldn't read him at all.

"Then you're not here looking for him?" she asked.

"I came over to retrieve a rake I lent to Mrs. Dorman. I'm still cleaning up in the garden from the storm that blew through last week."

Sydney's gaze flicked to the wall of tools behind him. His excuse was much better than hers. He probably had come over to grab his rake. Her mind raced as he turned and walked over to one of the hooks. What was it Trent had said when he came to visit her in the ER? Act like you belong, and people are generally reluctant to question you.

She tried to stand straighter, but the crutches made it difficult. "I came over to talk to him about his online writing class. I guess I'll have to catch him later."

Instead of retreating with the garden tool, Martin positioned himself between her and the door. His posture and demeanor were nonthreatening, but a warning shiver stole up her spine just the same. After all, how well did she really know him? She'd lived in his garage apartment for two years, but they didn't socialize. And she wasn't aware of anyone else in town who seemed to know much about him, despite the fact that he'd owned property in Seaside for more than thirty years. By every indication, he'd kept to himself even before his wife had died. His solitary lifestyle was certainly no indictment, but it made her current uneasiness somewhat understandable.

"An online writing class?" He dropped the rake to his side. "Are you sure you didn't misunderstand him?"

"No, he was very clear about it. I'm surprised he never mentioned it to you. I must say, I find it very exciting living next door to a writer."

"Yes, well…" He cleared his throat. "I'm sure he finds it equally as exciting to have a police detective next door."

She shifted on the crutches and gave him an ironic smile. "Not that I would be of much help these days. Anyway, as I was saying, he invited me to join his class when we met yesterday. I just dropped by to tell him that I've decided to take him up on the offer. It'll give me something to do while I'm out of commission with this ankle. When I came through the hedge, I noticed that the side door to the garage was open, and I thought he might be in here working."

Martin's gaze shifted to the freezer. "You said you were checking on something."

She gave him a contrite smile. "I was, but most people would call it just plain snooping. Please don't tell Mrs. Dorman."

"I'm not in contact with Mrs. Dorman, but I don't imagine she'd appreciate anyone poking through her private things." His tone altered almost infinitesimally, going from semi-cordial to slightly accusing.

Sydney winced. "Of course not. I should know better, and I'll be sure and offer an apology when I see her. This is no excuse, but I couldn't help wondering why someone who lives alone would need so much storage space. Mrs. Dorman is tiny and the freezer is massive. You could easily accommodate a side of beef in that thing… Or a body if you were so inclined." When he didn't respond to Sydney's macabre quip, she muttered, "Sorry. Cop humor."

"Yes, well—"

She cut him off before he could end the conversation. "Speaking of Mrs. Dorman's belongings, do you know what happened to her plants and pottery collection? She used to keep them on the shelves in her sunroom. They seemed to have disappeared."

He looked surprised. "You've been inside the house since she left?"

"No, but I noticed they were missing in one of the videos Brandon posted. Just seemed odd to me that she would pack them all up or give them away when she's only going to be gone a short time."

"I wouldn't know anything about that."

"You don't know anything about her missing possessions, or you don't know when she'll be back?"

"Either." He shifted the rake to his other hand, and whether consciously or not, he mimicked her leaning stance with the crutches.

Sydney kept her tone conversational as she probed. "I'm surprised she didn't share her schedule with you. Aren't you the one who arranged the short-term lease agreement with Brandon?"

"I played a very small role. She happened to mention a few days ago that she would be away for a while. She was worried about finding a house sitter and asked if I'd mind keeping an eye on the place. That's the only reason I got involved."

"I wonder why she didn't come to me," Sydney mused.

"You spend long hours at work. Or you did before the accident. I'm home all day. I would notice any strange cars or suspicious activity around the premises."

She nodded. "That makes sense."

"I knew..." He faltered. "Brandon was looking for a place to lease for the summer, so I gave Mrs. Dorman his number. They worked out the terms themselves. I had nothing to do with the arrangement."

Sydney's ears perked up at his hesitation. She started to ask about a pen name or alias, but something held her back. Martin Swann had always been unfailingly polite to her, and more importantly, he was a conscientious landlord. She'd never thought twice about being alone with him, but for some reason, her guard had gone up the moment she'd turned to find him behind her.

He was the only one who knew her immediate whereabouts. The overhead door to the garage was still closed, so no one could see in from the street. She was suddenly all too aware of her isolated surroundings and the impediment of a broken ankle. And the fact that Martin had armed himself with a heavy-duty steel rake with sharp tines. What if he tried to stop her from leaving? What if he knocked her in the head or stabbed her and stuffed her body in the freezer? How long before anyone would find her?

She tried to shake off the notion. No reason in the world to even think such a thing, yet her mind still went there. For a moment, she let herself imagine how she would defend herself, given her injuries. She could use one of the crutches to disarm him or even as a bludgeon if it came to it. A well-placed chop to the knees or groin could halt if not incapacitate him.

But why on earth would Martin Swann attack her when he'd never shown the slightest inclination for violence or even confrontation?

All this raced through her mind as she smiled pleasantly. "Regardless, I'm sure Mrs. Dorman appreciated the effort. It's probably reassuring to her that you know Brandon personally. He told me the two of you go way back. He said he and his family lived in this house for a time when he was a kid. You made such an impression that he still calls you Uncle Marty."

She sensed that same strange tension she'd noticed the day before when he delivered her printer. It wasn't fear or even disapproval, but a kind of wary excitement. She told herself now would be a good time to make her exit. For all she knew, Detective Bertram's car might already be waiting for her at the curb. That was some comfort. If she didn't turn up soon, she'd surely get a call or text.

Instead, she continued to try and draw him out. She told herself she wouldn't be much of a detective if she allowed this opportunity to pass her by. Wasn't that the purpose of her foray into Brandon Shaw's private domain? To find out all she could about her enigmatic neighbor?

"He told me he's always wanted to come back and spend more time in Seaside. He's looking forward to the peace and quiet of a small town. Nothing to do but fish and swim. His words."

Martin said in a strained voice, "I'm afraid you're laboring under a misconception, Detective Shepherd. Or perhaps you've made an assumption. Donnie didn't live here with his family."

She lifted a brow. "Who's Donnie?"

"You know him as Brandon. Donnie was his nickname as a boy."

"If he didn't live here, then why did he tell me that he did?"

Martin sighed. "You should ask him. It really isn't my place."

She wasn't going to let him off the hook that easily. "I couldn't help noticing yesterday that you seemed a bit anxious in his presence."

"Not anxious. Cautious."

"Why?"

He glanced over his shoulder toward the open door. "I don't like talking out of turn…"

"Please speak your mind," Sydney encouraged when he trailed off. "There's no one here but us."

"I knew Donnie a long time ago, and circumstances can change after so many years. People change. I've always believed that everyone deserves a second chance."

She'd been a cop long enough to know that not everyone deserved a reprieve, but she merely nodded. "I won't say anything to him. You have my word."

"He lived here but not with his family. Not his real family," he hurried to add when she started to interrupt. "He and the other boys were sent here after their release from juvenile detention."

Sydney tried to hide her shock, though deep down, she wasn't really surprised. Despite his charm and affable demeanor, Brandon Shaw had a disturbing, disruptive air about him. "They lived with Mrs. Dorman?"

"This was before the Dormans bought the property and renovated. For a short time, the building was used as a halfway house for troubled youth. A place where adolescents could assimilate back into society before returning to their parents or to foster care. Or in some cases, back to juvenile detention."

"I had no idea." The revelations about Brandon Shaw were fascinating, but it was Martin's willingness to speak to her so candidly that floored Sydney. She couldn't remember him ever uttering more than a few sentences when she sought him out, let alone carrying on a mostly one-sided conversation. The topic of Brandon Shaw—Donnie— seemed to have triggered a need for disclosure.

"I'm not surprised you don't remember," he said. "It was a long time ago. The neighborhood has changed a lot over the years. People come and go. The elderly forget." His expression turned pensive. "I knew from the start that Brandon was different from the other boys. He was intelligent, charming and uncommonly clever. He'd been on his own for a long time, so he didn't respond well to the program or to being mentored."

"You were his mentor?"

"Unofficially, I suppose. Officially, the program used local volunteers. Teachers, businessmen, police officers. People in positions of authority. They devoted a lot of time and effort to the boys, but there is only so much that can be undone when the damage starts so early. Eventually, you have to accept the fact that some people are beyond help."

"Was Brandon?"

He glanced away. "I didn't think so at first. For whatever reason, he took a liking to me. He would follow me around the garden and soak up everything I taught him. He was like a sponge when a subject interested him. He liked working with his hands. He was a quick learner and a hard worker when he set his mind to it. My wife and I never had children of our own, so I enjoyed spending time with him. I hoped I could eventually make a difference, but…" He sighed. "He still had so much to learn when the halfway house was shut down and the boys were sent away. It was a shame what happened."

"What did happen?"

He gave her an enigmatic look. "Before I continue, I want you to understand something."

She nodded.

"I don't like gossip. I mind my own business and I expect others to do the same. I'm telling you about the past for a reason." His pause was nearly imperceptible. "You're a young woman alone. You have a right to know who's living next door to you."

A thrill tingled down her spine. She didn't bother pointing out her profession or denying her current vulnerabilities. She merely nodded. "I appreciate that."

"I used to travel for my work two or three nights a week. Once, while I was away, Donnie and another boy broke into our house. My wife woke up and caught them going through our things. They were looking for cash, most likely. They grew aggressive when she confronted them. They didn't hurt her, but she was badly frightened."

"Did she file a report?"

"She wanted to, but I was afraid a visit from the police would only escalate the situation. She agreed, though she didn't want Donnie coming around anymore. I didn't blame her. I told him he had betrayed my trust, and now he had to keep his distance."

"How did he take it?"

"Not well. He said some unkind things about my wife, but I let it go. I was afraid he might try to cause even more trouble, so I postponed travel as much as I could. A few weeks after the incident, the halfway house closed down. The windows and doors were boarded up, and the boys just disappeared overnight. Turns out, some of the other neighbors had been complaining."

"What happened to Brandon?"

"I never knew. Truth be told, I didn't want to know."

"You didn't keep in touch?"

"Not for several years. As he grew older, he would occasionally send a card to let me know how he was getting on. I never responded and I didn't tell my wife. His messages were brief but sometimes troubling. Reading between the lines, he seemed to be taunting me."

"Taunting you how?"

"Vague nuances and innuendos. I thought it best to sever ties completely."

"Did you keep the cards?"

"I burned them as soon as I read them. I didn't want to take the chance that Margaret would find them. She was sick and frail by that time. I wanted to spare her any worry. Hers was a gradual decline but devastating nonetheless."

"I'm sorry for your loss," Sydney murmured.

"No need to be sorry. The end was a blessing for both of us." He took another long breath and released it slowly, as if to expel any residual despair or regret. "A few months after she died, he showed up on my doorstep. He must have been in his early twenties by that time. He seemed different. He wanted to be called Brandon, but his name wasn't the only thing that had changed. He was no longer aggressive or rough around the edges, but a quiet, thoughtful, humble young man. Still charming, of course, and so personable I couldn't find it in me to send him away. I invited him back to the garden. I'm not sure why. Loneliness, I suppose. I did enjoy his company that day. We talked for hours. He seemed genuinely distressed to hear about Margaret. And then he told me the most fantastic story."

Sydney had long since forgotten about the waiting car, the imminent meeting with Lieutenant Bertram and the missing white sandals. She had only a passing thought for Trent and his mission at the storage unit. She ignored her surroundings and the very real possibility that Brandon Shaw could return at any moment. Far better—and safer— to continue the conversation on the other side of the hedge, but she didn't want to give Martin an opportunity to have second thoughts.

"What did he tell you that day?"

"He said he'd located his birth parents through DNA testing. One of those public databases where people can learn about their heritage or search for long-lost relatives. He never knew anything about the circumstances of his birth. He'd been placed in foster care as an infant. He found out his mother was dead, but his father was very much alive, and he agreed to see him. Evidently, he was—is—a very successful businessman. He offered to help Brandon financially, even going so far as to set up a trust fund. I thought he was exaggerating at first. It sounded too good to be true. But his car and clothing looked expensive, and the changes in him were profound."

"Did he tell you who his father is?"

"No, and I never asked. I had a feeling the man's generosity came with a price."

"What do you mean?"

Martin shrugged. "Someone with status and a reputation to maintain might view a long-lost son as an inconvenience. Particularly one with a troubled past."

"You think he bought Brandon's silence?"

"That was my suspicion."

"Is Brandon Shaw even his real name?"

"I only knew him as Donnie. I never heard a last name. The young man you know as Brandon Shaw is very handsome and charismatic. Even as a boy, he had a disarming personality. I'm happy for him if he's truly turned his life around, but you've heard the old saying about a leopard changing its spots."

"You said you believe in second chances."

"In theory, yes, but I also worry that some people can't change their innate nature." He glanced once more over his shoulder as if sensing someone outside. Then he picked up the rake and slung it over his shoulder. "I wouldn't come over here alone if I were you. And I'd be very careful who I let into my apartment."

THE CHANGE TO his whiteboard continued to plague Trent as he left Sydney's neighborhood and headed to the storage unit on the other side of town. His mind drifted back to that moment last night when he'd discovered the subtle addition to his map followed by the dreaded certainty that the killer had been inside his house. He'd come in through a window while Trent had sat only yards away on the patio watching the water. He'd stood in Trent's office studying the series of blue x's that visually represented his seven-year killing spree. He may even have thrilled to the notion that his work was being researched, analyzed and—in his mind—admired after so many years. And then, before going out the same way he'd come in, he'd left a puzzling yet chilling clue. A tiny black cross had been added to the map in permanent marker.

The modification was so slight that Trent could have easily overlooked the icon had he not been familiar with every nuance of that map. But it was where the symbol had been placed that mattered. It was what that particular addition potentially represented that even now turned his veins to ice.

The line of blue x's along the I-45 corridor represented the seven original homicides, and the three red x's clustered around the Seaside area denoted the most recent murders. The cross had been placed to the left—west on the map— of the blue *x* that designated the location of where the fifth victim had been discovered. Tom Shepherd had been the lead investigator on that case and had later brought in the FBI to advise, profile and widen the search.

So, why a cross? Not an *x* like the other markers, but a distinct symbol denoting a possible grave. Was the killer trying to tell him that he'd already killed again and that he'd buried the body in the same wooded area where the fifth victim had been found? Or was the goal to send him on a wild-goose chase?

The notion crossed Trent's mind that Sydney's initial suggestion might be spot on. A fan of his podcast had become a little too obsessed and wanted to get his attention by playing a macabre game of cat and mouse. But that didn't explain the bloodstained scarf. Would a fan go so far as to break into his house and plant a fake clue on his map? Or cruise the bay night after night, stopping in the same location precisely at midnight? Who would have that kind of dedication?

Instead of heading straight to the storage unit as planned, Trent drove to the edge of town and pulled onto a gravel service road. The wooded area on either side of the narrow lane served as a median between Seaside's industrial area and the interstate. Directly behind him was a row of rundown warehouses, many of them abandoned. In front of him, a metal fence kept motorists from cutting through to the freeway, but he could easily climb over the gate.

He sat peering down the road and into the trees as he consulted his mental map and got his bearings. Dark clouds gathered overhead, and it had started to sprinkle. If he was going to do this, he needed to get a move on before the heavy rain set in.

Chamber-checking his Glock, he got out of the vehicle and stuffed the weapon in his jeans as he glanced over his shoulder to make sure no passersby had spotted him. Scanning the rows of warehouse windows, he could imagine someone standing in one of the vacant spaces watching him. The hair at his nape bristled, but he ignored the sensation as he scaled the gate and paused on the other side to survey his surroundings. The freeway was only half a mile or so straight ahead, but the trees buffered the traffic noise. He might have been miles from civilization, the silence was so complete.

Without sunlight streaming down through the tree branches, the woods seemed thick and oppressive. Or maybe the sense of doom came more from the mystery of what he might find rather than his surroundings. He wondered again about the significance of the cross. For all he knew, he could be walking into a trap. The symbol could represent death, all right. His.

Senses on full alert, he walked deeper into the gloom. Twenty-two years ago, the killer had traversed this same unpaved road. An experienced predator by then with at least four murders under his belt, he'd come in from the freeway side of the woods, using a bolt cutter to open the gate. He'd parked his vehicle on the side of the road and dragged the victim's body into the woods. He hadn't bothered digging even a shallow grave but instead had left her to the elements. A few days later, a motorist who had run out of gas on the interstate found her on his way into town. He'd spotted her right shoe lying in the ditch, along with tire tracks and footprints that had led him to search the immediate area where he soon discovered the body. The fifth victim's death had been the first of three consecutive strangulations. In Trent's estimation, her murder marked an important transition for the killer.

The FBI profiler had theorized that the diverse MO in the four previous murders was a deliberate misdirection by a cunning monster who knew how to mask his identity along with his true nature. A killer so clever that he varied his modus operandi, the location of his murders and his victim criteria in order to fool and elude the police. The profiler determined that they were looking for a male unsub, probably in his late twenties to late thirties—mobile, adaptive and patient. The killer knew how to blend in rather than call attention to himself. And he'd known when to call it quits.

Trent had developed a slightly different theory after he'd interviewed members of the victims' families and some of the detectives who'd worked those early cases. The killer had been clever and cunning, no doubt about that. But he'd also been experimenting and evolving, searching for the perfect method of taking a life that would reward him with the greatest thrill and the longest high.

Strangulation gave him the opportunity to prolong death by easing and increasing pressure on the victim's veins and arteries. It required no special tools or cleanup, and the foreplay could last as long as he wanted. He alone could choose the time of death. Gazing into his victim's eyes, he could relish every moment of her struggle, teasing and tormenting before succumbing to an obscene pleasure as the fight left her body and the light in her eyes faded.

The moment the fifth victim died, the Seaside Strangler had been born. He'd killed twice more in the same manner, and then for whatever reason, he'd gone to ground. Maybe he realized his time was limited. The consistency of his new MO gave him the greatest thrill, but it also put him at risk because it created a pattern. And patterns were too easily traced.

The three recent murders were still a puzzle to Trent. He hadn't yet worked out how everything fit together. Possibly the killer's appetite for taking lives had grown more voracious during his dormancy. That could explain the escalation. Three kills in less than a year.

Or maybe a second younger predator had brought the Seaside Strangler out of hiding to defend his territory. Maybe he didn't appreciate someone invading his turf, muddying his history, stealing his perfected method of death.

But why would the killer contact you? Sydney had asked in response to his explanation about the scarf. Only one person could answer that question, but Trent had a theory about that, too. If the recent murders had awakened a latent hunger, his podcast had stroked the killer's ego. He no longer wanted to blend in; he wanted notoriety on his terms. He wanted his story told. He wanted a legacy.

By this time, Trent was far down the service road and had long since abandoned any thought of turning back. The sprinkles had turned into a light shower. The air felt thick and cloying, but the rain was refreshing. He knew from his many conversations with Doug Carter where the fifth body had been found.

Look for a metal rod in the ground on the left side of the road coming in from town. Tom Shepherd placed that marker years ago. From there go straight into the woods maybe ten or fifteen yards. You should find what's left of a memorial. The last time I talked to Tom, he said he still went out there from time to time to throw away the dead flowers and tidy up around the place. I think those visits somehow made him feel closer to the victim. And I think he harbored a small hope that he would someday run into the killer.

Trent located the iron rod without any trouble and took a left into the woods. He could see the faint remnants of a path where people had once trekked through the trees to visit the area. Seemed a little strange to him. The victim hadn't drawn her last breath or been laid to rest in that spot. Instead, her lifeless body had been dumped and left to the vultures. But maybe that was the purpose of the memorial—to remind people that she was more than a victim, more than a number, more than a vicious killer's prey. She'd been a human being. Someone's daughter, sister, lover, friend.

The deeper into the woods he walked, the quieter his surroundings. He heard nothing at all except for the patter of rain on the leaves. Every now and then he stopped to listen, just to make sure he wasn't so inured in the quiet that he missed the snap of a twig or a footfall. He didn't think he'd been followed. He was adept at spotting tails, but he'd also been a little preoccupied. Not good. He was out here alone, basically at the invitation of a killer. He needed to stay focused.

Shaking off his disquiet, he moved farther along the path, eventually stepping out of the woods into a small clearing. He knew immediately he was in the right place. No mistaking the makeshift altar of stones.

The flowers that had been placed on top of them had long since withered, and the stuffed animals scattered on the ground had lost eyes, ears and stuffing to time and inclement weather. But someone had visited the altar recently. Trent spotted footprints in the damp earth.

The breeze picked up, rattling dead leaves across the clearing. Thunder rumbled in the distance, and he wondered how long he had before the clouds cracked open in earnest. He told himself to get back to the car and touch base with Sydney. He needed to tell her about the break-in at his house the previous evening and the addition of the cross to his map. He needed to make sure she was okay, because he had a very bad feeling they'd misjudged something important.

Instead of listening to that internal warning, he walked slowly around the clearing, looking for signs of fresh digging. Then he hunkered in front of the altar, careful to avoid the footprints, and sifted through the offerings for clues. He was so absorbed in the task that a sudden movement caught him by surprise. His head jerked skyward as a flock of grackles took flight. Something other than the approaching storm had startled them from their roosts.

Someone was coming toward him through the woods.

Chapter Eight

The premature twilight had brought out the predators. Somewhere behind Trent, a barn owl screamed a warning. His spine tingled even as he recognized the eerie sound from the summers he'd spent on his grandparents' farm in East Texas. Deep in the country with no neighbors for miles, the high-pitched screech had been terrifying to a six-year-old boy. To this day, the sound reminded him nothing so much as an uncanny combination of a child in distress, a mythical banshee and the velociraptors from a popular movie.

Feeling exposed, he took cover at the edge of the clearing, positioning himself so that he could keep an eye on the altar and the tree line directly across from him.

The owl screamed again, sending that same icy finger down his backbone. He drew his weapon and kept it at his side. With his other hand, he silenced his ringtone, but he didn't put the phone away. For some reason, he had an almost urgent need to touch base with Sydney. What if he'd been lured out here so that she would be left alone? An absurd notion. He'd come here on impulse. No way the killer could have predicted his plans. Still...

He thumbed a text:

Everything okay?

Her reply was immediate:

Just now getting to the station. I'll let you know how it goes.

He wasn't about to tell her that a killer might be stalking him in the woods, so he typed, Meet back at your place later?

When she sent an okay emoji, he added, Go straight home. Lock your door. Don't let anyone in until I get there.

?????

I'll explain when I see you. Be careful.

He pocketed his phone as he scanned the clearing.

All was silent now. The owl seemed to have scared away the wildlife. No birds took flight. No small creatures scurried through the underbrush to safety. It was as if everything that lived in the woods had gone into hiding. He listened intently for the telltale snap of a twig or the crunch of leaves underfoot, but the only sound he could distinguish was the distant hum of a car engine out on the freeway.

He drew a couple of long breaths to slow his pulse. Minutes went by. He wondered if he had imagined a presence. Probably shouldn't have sent that text. Sydney had enough to deal with without his overreaction. For all he knew, he was alone in the woods. And she was at the police station surrounded by cops. Safe for now. No need to worry. Time to take a few photos of the area and head back to the car.

Instead, he held his position. He'd been baited into coming out here for a reason. He let another few minutes go by before he eased through the woods, heading west. The location on the map put the marker halfway between the clearing and the freeway. He could still be walking into a trap, but he didn't like giving up. Even as he hardened his resolve, he found himself thinking, *Don't let me find a body.*

The farther west he walked, the louder the cars on the freeway. The swoosh of tires on wet pavement mingled with the rhythmic drumming of raindrops on the leaves. The sounds were normal, almost soothing, and he might have let down his guard except for the intrusion of another noise straight ahead of him in the trees. Rustling leaves. A snapped twig. The very signals he had been listening for earlier.

Trent paused. From the muted sounds, he'd judged the person to still be some distance away from him in the woods, yet he could have sworn he heard a hitched breath followed by a soft laugh.

Into the silence came the shrill screech of the owl. The uncanny scream seemed different this time, closer and more bloodcurdling. More human.

It's just an owl, he told himself, but in the next instant, he found himself scrambling through the vines and scrub brush, heedless of the noise he made and the thorns tearing at his ankles. Heedless of what might be waiting for him in the trees.

He warned himself to proceed with caution. Now was not the time to get careless. But what if the scream had come from someone in trouble? He couldn't ignore the possibility no matter how remote.

The rain slackened, but the trees continued to drip. His hair and shirt were soaked by the time he discovered a second clearing. He knew at once he'd found the spot that had been designated on his map. He stopped in his tracks, assuming a shooting stance as he lifted his weapon.

He did a quick scan of his surroundings before letting his gaze move more slowly around the clearing. In the center, a cross had been hammered into the damp ground. The two thin slats of wood had been crudely assembled, unpainted and unadorned except for a dead daisy chain draped over the horizontal arms. A bouquet of wilting white roses laid at the base.

Recognition dawned for Trent as adrenaline started to pump. White roses had been left in Sydney's hospital room after the accident. No way this could be a coincidence.

A connection to a killer who had been active when she was a little kid seemed implausible unless her speculation the previous night proved true. Had he known about her all along? Had he tormented her dad with vague threats and enigmatic clues the way he seemed intent on toying with Trent? Was this just a game to him, or was he working his way up to the next kill?

Trent started toward the cross only to freeze yet again as the feeling of being watched intensified. Someone was nearby, hiding in the bushes.

Scouring the shadows, he waited. Then, turning in a slow circle, he called out, "I know you're there. Who are you?"

No answer. Nothing stirred.

"What do you want?"

He kept his weapon steadied as he moved around the clearing, peering deep into the woods. "I've seen you on the water. You come every night at midnight. Why?"

Silence.

"Last night, you came ashore and broke into my house. You left a clue on my whiteboard. Why a cross? Why *this* cross? Is someone buried here?"

Another beat went by.

Trent's voice rose in frustration. "Coward! Show your-self! Tell me what you want!"

After a few minutes, the feeling of being watched faded. He listened intently for hints of a retreat. No sound came to him, yet his every instinct told him the danger had passed. He was once again alone in the woods.

Lowering his weapon to his side, he made another pass around the clearing, still probing the trees and underbrush for even the slightest movement.

He called out. "Are you there?"

The echo that came back to him seemed like a taunt. *Are you there, are you there, are you there?*

"Why have you been watching me?"

Watching me, watching me, watching me.

"Why run away? Are you afraid of me? You should be. I don't give up easily. Sooner or later, I'll find you."

If the killer still lingered in the woods, the thrown gaunt-let should have brought him out into the open.

You're losing it, Trent chided himself. Maybe he'd let his imagination and the desire to catch a killer get the better of him. Make his trek out here had been nothing more than the wild-goose chase he'd feared. But he wasn't imagining the cross or the white roses. Or the dead daisy chain that somehow seemed both sad and ominous.

He continued to circle, muttering questions to himself if for no other reason than to remain focused. "Why did you bring me here? What did you want me to see? The cross? The white roses?"

His head came back up to scour the tree line. His instinct was to plunge into the woods in pursuit. But where to start? Should he keep moving toward the freeway or backtrack to his vehicle? The killer had eluded the police for decades by being both cunning and cautious. He was never going to be that easy to catch.

Tucking the gun in his jeans, Trent walked back to the center of the circle and knelt to examine the cross, checking along the slats of wood for clues before turning his attention to the bouquet of roses. Raindrops glistened on the snowy petals as he parted the stems.

A card had been tucked down among the blossoms. The rain had dampened the envelope and blurred the ink inside, but he could still make out the message: *See you soon, Sydney.*

SYDNEY SENSED AN odd energy in the squad room that afternoon. She wondered if word had already spread about Richard Mathison's lawsuit. A couple of her colleagues waved a greeting, but most kept their heads buried in paperwork or pretended to be engrossed in phone calls. She had to admit, the cold shoulder stung a bit. It was one thing to purposely keep to herself, quite another to be openly shunned.

Her own fault, she supposed. She'd never gone out of her way to cultivate friendships, so why would anyone pretend to have her back now?

Funny how things could go south so quickly. One anonymous phone call, one mistake in judgment, and her career as a detective for the Seaside Police Department was effectively over. No one would be sorry to see her go. A few might view her inevitable termination as an opportunity the way she had when Trent had been fired. He hadn't gone quietly. A part of her had come to admire his departing rant. Or at least to understand it. His assessment of the department and some of his colleagues had been brutal. Sydney would know because she'd been on the receiving end of his disdain.

As satisfying as it might be to go out in a blaze of glory, losing control wasn't her style. She didn't like exposing her vulnerabilities. If she had to imagine herself leaving the building for the last time, it would be with her head high and her dignity, if nothing else, intact.

Keeping her focus straight ahead, she navigated through the crowded desks in the squad room and started down the hallway to the lieutenant's office. She tapped on the glass panel and waited until he responded before opening the door and poking her head in. He was hunched over his desk, phone pressed to his ear. His deep scowl didn't bode well for the nature of their visit. He invited her in with a quick beckoning gesture, then pointed to the chairs across from his desk. She lowered herself onto the one farthest from the door, effectively putting herself in a corner where she could pretend to fade into the woodwork. Then she placed her crutches on the floor as quietly as she could manage so as not to interrupt his call.

While she waited, she surveyed his office. She'd been there many times for a myriad of reasons, yet the amount of furniture crammed into the room always amazed her. Large desk and credenza, printer stand, chairs, filing cabinets. And on the beige walls, clusters of framed pictures, maps and citations.

She tried to distract herself by focusing on a group photograph that included her dad, but her mind kept going back to Trent's enigmatic texts. He'd seen her just a few minutes prior to sending those messages, so why had he felt the need to issue such a dire warning? *Go straight home. Lock your door. Don't let anyone in until I get there.*

Something must have happened after he left her apartment. Maybe he'd found a significant clue among her dad's belongings, or maybe he'd somehow intuited her foray into Brandon Shaw's garage. Those would be some serious precognitive abilities. More likely, he'd made an educated guess based on what he knew about her personality. It didn't take special powers to deduce that sooner or later, she was bound to investigate the premises next door.

She checked her phone. No additional texts or voicemails. His silence should have reassured her, but it didn't. She wondered what the lieutenant would think of her concern for Trent Gannon. An association with the former detective might be the final straw for him.

The lieutenant finished his call and made a few notes on a yellow legal pad before he glanced up. "Sorry about that. It's been one of those days."

She nodded and tried to relax, but instead she found herself sitting straighter as her fingers curled around the arms of the chair. Maybe it was her imagination, but the sound of voices and ringing telephones filtering in from the squad room seemed more chaotic than usual. *What the heck is going on around here?*

"Syd?"

She tried to shake off her trepidation. "Sorry. What?"

"Thanks for coming in on such short notice." He nodded toward her cast. "Can't be easy to get around with a broken ankle. Those stairs outside your apartment must be a bear."

"They're not so bad. You get the hang of it after a time or two. Besides, I didn't think I had a choice."

He folded his arms as he regarded her across the desk. "Of course you had a choice. It was a request not a summons."

"Isn't a request from your boss the same as a summons?"

"That's your interpretation, I guess. Regardless, I appreciate the effort. I wanted you to hear this from me before word gets out."

Her stomach sank as she gripped the armrests. "I have a

pretty good idea of why I'm here, so no need to beat around the bush. If I'm being terminated or demoted, just say so. I'd rather get it over with."

His expression remained annoyingly passive. "You think I asked you down here to fire you?"

She gave him a puzzled frown. "Didn't you? I heard Richard Mathison's press conference yesterday. His ultimatum was crystal clear. Either I go or he files a lawsuit against the department. I just assumed—"

Before the lieutenant could confirm or deny her suspicions, they were interrupted by a sharp rap on the door. Instead of inviting the person in, he got up and went over to answer. The chatter from the squad room filtered in through the open door. The commotion had a frenzied edge that made her wonder again if something major was about to go down. And if the pending event somehow involved her.

He closed the door and came back around to his desk. His brow remained deeply furrowed as he took a seat and swiveled around to face her once again.

Sydney glanced over her shoulder. "What's going on out there? Is it my imagination, or does everyone around here seem more tense than usual?"

His voice lowered to a gruff rumble. "It's not your imagination. There's a lot of buzz about an arrest."

"Must be a big bust. Since when does an apprehension generate this kind of excitement?"

He cleared his throat and straightened the papers on his desk, but his gaze never left hers. "Since it involves Gabriel Mathison. He was brought in on suspicion of murder."

For a moment, Sydney thought she must have misheard. Then her mouth dropped in astonishment. She was so taken aback she could only manage a monosyllabic response. "When?"

"A little while ago. He's still being booked. As you can imagine, everyone is a little on edge."

Sydney sat back in her chair as a myriad of emotions poured over her. Anger, first and foremost. Disappointment, betrayal, disbelief. Not two days after her suspension, the main suspect in a controversial and exhaustive investigation had been arrested, depriving her of the satisfaction of placing him in cuffs and closing her first murder case. She couldn't help but wonder if this had all been carefully orchestrated to take her down a peg or two. Maybe even to drive her out of the department. She thought about Trent's warning that once the wagons started to circle, no one would have her back.

She glanced at the closed door. No wonder the squad room was in an uproar. Gabriel Mathison in custody was big news, and everyone at the station was probably bracing for the fallout.

The lieutenant's gaze narrowed as if he didn't trust her silence. "Well? Aren't you going to say anything?"

She took a breath and counted to ten. "Why now? Why so soon after you took me off the case? You made it clear that Gabriel Mathison was off limits."

"He was off limits to you. He still is. You were suspended because of your reckless behavior. A full investigation is pending. Gabriel Mathison's arrest doesn't change anything in that regard. But he never stopped being a suspect. We just didn't have enough evidence to arrest him until today."

"What changed?"

"Turns out, his alibi isn't as airtight as he led us to believe."

"Let me guess," she said. "One of his friends finally turned on him."

"In a manner of speaking. Instead of partying in the VIP room until four in the morning as he and his buddies previously claimed, we have a witness who says Gabriel left the club shortly before midnight and was gone for over an hour. When he came back, he was visibly agitated. He started knocking back shots and grew more obnoxious and aggressive as the night wore on. The timeline comports with your witness's recanted claim that she saw Gabriel and Jessica in a loud altercation in the parking lot of her apartment complex around midnight."

"What did you mean, 'in a manner of speaking'?"

He paused as if considering how much he should tell her. It was obvious he wanted to keep her away from the case. It was also apparent that he wanted to maintain control by doling out just enough information to keep her from digging on her own.

"The witness didn't come forward of his own volition. He was picked up on a third-offense DWI. Which means he could be facing prison time with hardcore criminals instead of lockup in the county jail with a bunch of drunks. He's talking because he hopes the DA will take his cooperation into consideration."

"Do you think he's credible?"

"As credible as anyone looking to save his own hide. As of now, he's one piece of the puzzle, but he's not the only piece. We also received a tip from an anonymous caller who placed Gabriel's car—or one like it—near the area where Jessica's body was found. The caller said the vehicle was parked on the shoulder of the road with the trunk open. He stopped to offer assistance and saw what appeared to be blood on the driver's shirt. The driver claimed he'd been changing a flat. The jack slipped and cut his hand. The caller said he was only now reporting what he'd seen weeks ago because he recognized Gabriel Mathison from the press conference yesterday."

"Does Gabriel have a cut on his hand?"

"No, but a superficial injury would have had time to heal by now."

"Were you able to trace the call?"

"The caller used a burner. All we could get was a general location from where the call was placed."

"Hmmm." Sydney thought about that for a moment. "Why would someone go to the trouble of buying a disposable phone to call in a tip?"

"Obviously someone who doesn't want to get involved with the police."

"I guess, but all these things lining up at the same time strikes me as a little too convenient," she insisted. "I spent weeks investigating this case and pretty much hit a brick wall at every turn."

He gave her a look she couldn't decipher. She had to wonder what was going through his head at the moment. Just two days ago, he'd lectured her own the virtue of knowing when to back off only to end up arresting her main suspect. She wanted to take satisfaction in being proven right, but something seemed off about Gabriel Mathison's arrest. The timing bugged her as Trent's theory continued to niggle. *What if you're both wrong?*

"I don't know about convenient." The lieutenant's response drew her back to the conversation. "Murder cases aren't solved overnight. Sometimes weeks, months or even years go by before an investigation clicks into place. All it takes is for one person to come forward. Or in this case, two. We may not have a smoking gun yet, but we were able to obtain a warrant to search Gabriel's car. We found traces of hair and blood on a lug wrench stored beneath the carpet in the spare tire compartment. The lab results haven't come back yet, but if the blood matches the victim's DNA, then that tire iron may well be the murder weapon."

"Or it could prove he actually did cut his hand changing a flat." She was only too aware of how their roles had reversed. Since when had she become Gabriel Mathison's advocate? Since the evidence against him seemed a little too pat, she decided. "If the lug wrench was used to knock Jessica unconscious, why would he stuff it back in his trunk?"

He seemed confused by her attitude and rightfully so. "He probably meant to dispose of it somewhere away from the body but, in his agitated state, forgot to throw it out."

"That's a pretty important thing to forget," Sydney said. "How did he explain it?"

"As you would expect, he claims he's being set up."

"By whom?" When he hesitated, she said, "By me? That's ridiculous! How would I have gained access to his trunk?"

"Don't take it personally. He and his attorneys have been throwing around a lot of wild accusations. But at least he finally owned up to leaving the club around midnight. He also admitted to an altercation with Jessica in the parking lot, but he swears she was alive when he left her apartment complex. He says the tire iron must have been planted in his car at a later date."

Sydney tried to remain focused, but the conversation wasn't going at all as she'd expected. Now that she'd managed to tamp down her initial indignation, she was starting to ponder other possibilities. "The nightclub has valet parking. It's conceivable someone took his key fob from the stand and planted the blood in his trunk."

"Someone as in...?"

"Whoever killed Jessica King."

He cocked his head and tugged at his ear. "Hold on a second. I must be hearing things. For a minute there, I thought you said, 'whoever killed Jessica King.' I know that can't be right, because you're the person who insisted for weeks that Gabriel Mathison was our man."

"I know. Believe me, it's weird being on the other side of things. But I can't get past the timing. Two witnesses coming forward at virtually the same time? And what about the other two unsolved homicides? Both strangulations, both bodies found within miles of the Mathison beach home. If someone wanted to frame Gabriel, that's exactly where they'd dump the bodies."

He shook his head in disbelief. "This about-face is making my head spin. What happened since I saw you in the hospital? Two days ago, you were more convinced than ever that Gabriel Mathison was a cold-blooded killer. Not just a killer, but a predator. Now you sound like his attorney. Did he get to you? Did he threaten you somehow?"

"Yes, as a matter of fact he did, but that has nothing to do with my uncertainty regarding his arrest. And for the record, I still think he's a predator. His history of violent behavior speaks for itself. However, information has recently been brought to my attention that has made me question whether or not he's a murderer."

"What information?"

She leaned forward, her pulse quickening in apprehension. "What if I told you that someone credible has come to me with a compelling alternative theory? A premise that links all three murders to a killer who went dormant twenty years ago."

He didn't look impressed. "I'd say you've got too much time on your hands. You need to find a more productive hobby until that ankle heals."

"I know it sounds implausible. I discounted it, too, at first. But just hear me out for a minute." She sat back in her chair and tried not to let his attitude deflate her. He'd been a cop when the original seven murders occurred. He might remember something valuable if she could keep him sufficiently engaged. "Do you remember a series of murders that occurred in the late 1990s to the early 2000s here in Southeast Texas? The bodies of seven young women were found in as many years along the interstate from Houston to Galveston. My dad was lead detective on one of those cases. He was the first investigator to suspect a single killer in all seven cases, and he eventually called in the FBI for support."

The lieutenant fiddled with a pen as he turned to glance out the window. He seemed distracted and not very interested in pursuing an alternative theory. "I remember the murders, but I never agreed with the single-killer theory. There were too many disparities. A lone perpetrator never made any sense to me, and I told Tom so. But he wouldn't listen to reason. No one's opinion mattered but his own. We even had a brief falling out over it."

She said in surprise, "I never knew that."

He shrugged. "We both got over it. We put all that business behind us when we became partners. Tom was the smartest detective I ever worked with, but he wasn't infallible. For whatever reason, he became obsessed with those murders. He lost all perspective. It was like he had a personal vendetta to carry out."

"What do you mean?"

"The investigation consumed so much of his time and attention that he let it become personal. Every cop has a case like that in the course of a long career. The one that gets away. The one that eats at you for years. Tom convinced himself there was an active serial killer in the area and that he alone could catch him. The righteous crusader complex. He never gave up looking until the day he died."

There was an edge of disdain in the lieutenant's description that didn't sit well with Sydney. "If he was so obsessed, why did he never talk about those cases at home? He never even mentioned them to me after I became a cop."

"Maybe he didn't want you taking up his lost cause."

She frowned at that. "You do know the FBI validated his theory. When they correlated the casefiles, they found a common link."

"You mean the missing shoes." His tone remained dismissive.

"A missing left shoe in every single case," Sydney stressed. "Do you really think that was a coincidence?"

"What I think is that shoes are the first articles of clothing to go missing when a body is stuffed in a trunk or dragged through the woods. Nothing coincidental or unusual about it."

"But a left shoe is specific," she insisted.

He sighed. "The press got that whole thing started after the first woman was grabbed leaving a New Year's Eve party. One of her fancy shoes was found in the parking garage after she went missing. A blue high heel with a crystal bow on the toe. I remember the details because every newspaper in the area ran a color photo of that shoe on the front page with a caption about a missing Cinderella. That was before social media took over our lives, but the photograph found its way into dozens if not hundreds of chat rooms and message boards. The national news even picked it up for a minute, but you know how those things go. A week later, something else captured the public's attention."

Sydney grew even more insistent. "Don't you think it's

possible the killer enjoyed the notoriety so much that he started collecting shoes as trophies from his victims?"

"Anything's possible, but I think it more likely that the idea of a missing shoe was already planted in Tom's head when he started trying to connect the cases."

"The FBI, as well?"

"Your dad could be extremely persuasive. And tunnel vision happens to the best of us. I think they all found what they wanted to find." He gave her a long scrutinizing look. "I can't help wondering who planted the idea in your head."

"Why does that matter?"

"It matters if you've been talking to Trent Gannon."

She gaped in astonishment. "How could you possibly know that?"

He sat back in his chair, still eyeing her with the same speculative expression. "I've listened to his podcast from time to time. He's all about digging through old casefiles and trying to poke holes in the original investigations to prove his superior detective skills. He comes across as a guy with an axe to grind."

Sydney started to protest, but she didn't want to sound overly defensive or too invested. Instead, she said casually, "I was surprised to learn he even had a podcast. He never struck me as the type. How long have you been listening?"

"On and off for a couple of years, mostly out of curiosity."

"You never said anything."

"Why would I bring up some random podcast?" The lieutenant was still fiddling with the pen, but he no longer seemed distracted. Sydney had a feeling he might be more engrossed in the conversation than he wanted to reveal. "For the past couple of weeks, he's been focusing on the seven cases you just mentioned. He even managed to drag a retired detective onto his show, and I hear he's been talking to other law enforcement personnel who were involved in some of those investigations. Considering your dad's role in the single killer fantasy, I figured it was only a matter of time before he contacted you."

"Have you talked to him?" she asked curiously.

"No. The murders occurred before Tom and I were partners." He glanced up. "Whatever he said must have been convincing if he's made you second-guess Gabriel Mathison's guilt."

"I'm just trying to keep an open mind," she said. "Three unsolved strangulations twenty years ago. Three more strangulations in the past year. I can't help but see a pattern." She wondered what he would say about the bloodstained scarf and the midnight boat sightings. As much as she wanted to observe his reaction, she wouldn't go behind Trent's back.

The lieutenant continued to watch her from across his desk. The vibe in the office had changed since she first entered. The look on his face wasn't disappointment or exasperation or even anger. He seemed guarded, as if he no longer felt comfortable in her company. She wondered if he resented the heat that had rained down on the department from her actions or if they were just naturally growing apart. Her dad had been the common bond, and he'd been gone for nearly five years. Without him, what did she have in common with Dan Bertram except for their profession?

"A word of caution?"

She forced a brief smile and a nod. "Of course. I always appreciate your input."

"Whatever you think of Gabriel Mathison's arrest or anything else we've discussed today, keep it to yourself. Don't go around spouting alternative theories. In other words, don't make waves. Why give the review board an excuse to delay your reinstatement?" He paused with another hard scrutiny. "If you're smart, you'll stay away from Trent Gannon. There's a reason he's no longer a cop."

She kept her response neutral. "I appreciate your concern, but by every indication, he's turned his life around. His podcast is successful, and if he's found a niche solving cold cases, more power to him. He was once an excellent detective. Why should his talents go to waste?"

He didn't look pleased by her defense. "He's damaged goods, Syd. Don't make the mistake of thinking you can fix or even trust him. He's the kind of guy who will drag you down with him if you're not careful."

"I'll take that under advisement." She tried not to sound dismissive as she bent to retrieve her crutches, but working with Trent was her decision. She was anxious to get home and find out what he'd uncovered at the storage unit. Not to mention filling him in on what she'd learned from Martin Swann.

"Sit tight," the lieutenant said as he picked up the receiver. "I'll have someone drive you home."

"Thanks."

The conversation seemed to be ending on a strained note. Sydney couldn't help reflecting with a bit of nostalgia that their once close and oftentimes combative relationship had shifted into something more secretive and restrained.

While he made the call, she took out her own phone and glanced at the screen. Nothing new from Trent. She didn't know whether to be relieved or worried—

She jumped as the lieutenant replaced the receiver with a loud bang. Then she heard him mutter an oath a split second before the door to his office slammed against the wall so hard the glass panel rattled. He jumped to his feet, sending his desk chair flying back into the credenza.

Sydney was so taken aback by the commotion and his startled demeanor that she dropped her crutches, adding to the confusion. She braced herself against the back of the chair as Richard Mathison stormed through the door. The officer who trailed him tried to subdue him, but Richard shook him off and strode across the room to plant his hands on the lieutenant's desk, his rage so consuming he appeared oblivious to Sydney's presence.

"What the *hell* is going on around here?" he demanded.

The lieutenant cleared his throat. "I take it you've heard about the arrest."

"Did you think I wouldn't?"

"I'm a little surprised to see you so soon. Your assistant said you were away on a business trip."

"Well, that explains the timing." Venom dripped from Mathison's voice. "You waited until my back was turned, otherwise, you wouldn't have dared."

"If you'll calm down, I'll try to explain what happened." After the initial shock, the lieutenant managed to regain his composure. He rolled his chair back to the desk and sat down, straightened his phone and then clasped his hands on the surface.

Sydney's attention shifted back and forth between the two men. Richard Mathison was an imposing figure, though not so much physically. Like his son, he was an inch or two shy of six feet, slim and athletic with an imperious demeanor. But the gleam of cruelty in his eyes and the sneer of disdain in his voice had a chilling effect Sydney wasn't immune to. Despite her relentless pursuit of Gabriel Mathison these past few weeks, she found herself trying to shrink into the shadows. Her timidity annoyed her. She had to admire the lieutenant's comportment, but then, he wasn't without his own power.

Richard leaned in. "Maybe now is a good time to remind you of all the favors I've done for this department over the years. And for you."

The lieutenant gave a brief nod to the uniformed officer still hovering behind Mathison. The officer retreated into the hallway but left the door open and stationed himself just outside. Sydney wished she could slink out of the office behind him. On the other hand, she was riveted by Richard Mathison's words. What favors?

"Maybe now is a good time to remind you that no one is above the law," the lieutenant countered.

"Get off your high horse, Danny. We both know you've done your share of cutting corners and looking the other way...and worse. Gabriel has his faults, but he's no murderer. If nothing else, he wouldn't have the stomach for it. Until about a minute ago, you agreed with me."

"That was before new evidence came to light."

Richard straightened. "You mean the drunk trying to save his own skin or the anonymous phone call? No judge in his right mind would issue a search warrant on such flimsy evidence unless someone with influence twisted his arm. That had to be you or the chief, and I don't think she's that stupid."

"You're forgetting about the blood sample we collected from his car."

"Undoubtedly planted by one of your officers."

The lieutenant merely shrugged at the accusation. "If Gabriel is innocent, you have nothing to worry about."

"Innocent people get railroaded into prison every day. What I can't figure out is why you thought you could get away with framing him. You know me well enough to realize that an attack on my family is an attack on me."

"Is that a threat?"

"Wait and find out."

Sydney shivered as Gabriel's warning came back to her. *You have no idea what he's capable of.*

Despite that warning, something about the confrontation struck her as off. She couldn't put her finger on why. Then she chided herself for the suspicion, but she couldn't help eyeing both men with skepticism. She couldn't help remembering Trent's advice about watching her back when it came to Dan Bertram.

"I've given this a lot of thought," Richard was saying. "And I believe I've figured out your motivation. One, it gives you leverage against a lawsuit. And two, you're trying to protect someone. I've been asking myself who would have the most to gain by Gabriel's arrest. Who had access to the victim's DNA?"

The lieutenant's gaze darted to Sydney. Mathison had been so singularly focused on his attack that her presence had gone unnoticed. Whether unwittingly or otherwise, the lieutenant had just given her away.

Or had he?

Richard turned slowly, his knowing gaze meeting hers before taking in her cast and the crutches on the floor. "Well, well, well. If it isn't the erstwhile Detective Shepherd."

She returned his stare without flinching even though his unblinking inspection had thoroughly unnerved her. She tried to stand straighter without appearing to stand straighter. "Hardly erstwhile. I'm still a detective."

"I wouldn't count on being reinstated after this stunt," he said. "Planting evidence in my son's car took guts. I'll give you that. You remind me of your father. Smug and self-righteous but not nearly as bright as you think you are."

The mention of her dad shocked her. She automatically lashed out. "Don't talk about my dad."

His expression altered, hardened. "I'll talk about anyone I damn well please. Do you have any idea what you've unleashed?"

Before Sydney could utter a word in her defense or even steady her balance, he crossed the space between them in two strides. She sidestepped reflexively and her weight came down on her broken ankle. She would have tumbled to the floor if he hadn't grabbed her arms. From the lieutenant's vantage, it would look as if Mathison had caught her before she toppled, but the feral gleam in his eyes told her otherwise.

Blocking her with his body, he slid his hands over her shoulders and briefly cupped his fingers around her neck. He didn't squeeze. To the contrary, his touched was almost intimate.

Sydney shuddered in disgust even as his expression held her enthralled. Something dark flashed in his eyes as he ran his tongue over his lips. His fingers tightened almost imperceptibly, and then he released her with a knowing smile.

The lieutenant couldn't have seen that smile or Mathison's fingers around her neck. He didn't have any idea what had just passed between them in the blink of an eye. Sydney wasn't even certain herself. The one thing she did know— Richard Mathison was in complete control of his faculties. And he was enjoying himself immensely.

"Careful," he murmured. "We wouldn't want you to fall and hurt yourself again."

The moment he stepped back, Sydney's ankle gave way and she crumpled to the floor. He didn't try to help her up but instead turned his back to her. And the lieutenant didn't leap to her aid. For the longest moment, he merely stared down at her from behind his desk. She tried to give him the benefit of the doubt. Maybe he was still in shock from the confrontation.

But for a moment, she could have sworn he looked coldly indifferent to her pain.

Chapter Nine

Trent was sitting on the outside stairs when Sydney got home. He strode down the driveway as the squad car pulled to the curb to let her out. Despite everything that had happened at the station, she felt excited to see him and more than a little grateful that she didn't have to face an evening alone in her apartment.

She murmured her thanks as he helped her with the crutches. Then he closed the car door and put a steadying hand on her elbow until she had her balance. She'd learned at a very young age the importance of self-reliance and had always prided herself on her fierce independence. But she had to admit that every now and then, it was nice to have someone, literally, to lean on.

"You okay?" he asked as the officer drove away. "You look a little flushed."

"Just hot and sticky. The AC was out in the vehicle and the drive home seemed to take forever. We caught every traffic light." She teetered on one foot while she adjusted the crutches. "But I'm here now and I have so much to tell you. You won't believe all that's happened since you left the apartment earlier. It's been a wild afternoon."

"I have a lot to tell you, too, but you first. How did the meeting with Bertram go?" He reached up and absently tucked back a strand of hair that had blown loose from her ponytail. He didn't even seem conscious of the gesture, but Sydney's pulse jumped, and she had to suppress her reaction.

She swallowed. "He didn't fire me. At least, not yet. That's something, I guess."

"Then what was so urgent that he had to see you today?"

"It's kind of a long story. I'll tell you everything, I promise, but I'd like to go upstairs and freshen up before we get into it. I'm hot and grimy, and the squad car smelled like sweat and bad takeout. I need to wash my face and get something cold to drink." *And just sit for a minute and catch my breath.* The confrontation with Richard Mathison had left her shaken, particularly the dig at her dad. No doubt, that had been his intent. He'd instinctively known how to cut her to the quick.

If she concentrated too hard, she could still feel the touch of his hands around her neck, could still see that feral gleam in his eyes as his tongue flicked out to lick his lips in anticipation. She shuddered at the memory.

Her reaction didn't go unnoticed. Trent studied her features. "Are you sure you're okay?"

"Let's just get inside."

He checked their surroundings and gave a tense nod. "Good idea. I'll follow you up the stairs."

Once they reached the top, she unlocked the door and beckoned him in with a nod, but he lingered on the landing. "You go on in without me. Unless you need my help with something."

"I think I can manage a glass of ice water on my own. But…aren't you staying?" She tried to hide her disappointment. "We have a lot to talk about."

"I'll be right back. I just need to get something from the

car." When she waited for an explanation, he said, "I brought some boxes back from the storage unit. I hope you don't mind. I thought we could go through the contents together."

"I don't mind, but I'm surprised you had the patience to wait for me. Ever since you came to see me in the hospital, you've been champing at the bit to get your hands on my dad's files."

"Something came up. Another errand ate up my time, and I wanted to be here when you got back, so I did a quick search. You're right. Your dad was very detail-oriented, and he took copious notes. We can go back to the storage unit tomorrow and take another look, but the files I brought should keep us occupied for the rest of the evening."

Her first instinct was to press him about the other errand, not to mention the enigmatic text messages he'd sent earlier. Instead, she nodded and left him at the door. Plenty of time to get into all that later. Right now, she needed a moment alone to pull herself together. The ride home wasn't the only thing that had left her feeling grimy.

She shivered as she stood at the bathroom mirror and stared at her flushed reflection. Then, propping her crutches against the wall, she undid her collar so that she could examine her neck. No marks, of course. Mathison had applied just enough pressure to make her skin crawl. The image repelled her and made her queasy. Unclean. She bent to splash cold water on her face, and then she got out a washcloth to scrub her neck where she imagined the imprint of his fingers lingered.

What would have happened if he'd caught her alone? Would he have been able to restrict his anger to a taunt, or would he have wrapped his hands around her neck and squeezed the life from her?

And what was going on with Lieutenant Bertram? Why

had he hesitated so long to come to her aid when she fell? She hated to think that Trent could be right about him, but she was starting to wonder if she'd ever known the real Dan Bertram. Had her dad?

She had no idea how long she'd been in front of the mirror lost in thought when she spotted Trent's reflection. He stood in the living room staring down the short hallway at her.

"Sorry," he said when their gazes connected. "I didn't mean to intrude on your privacy. The door was open, and you looked upset."

"I'm fine. Just trying to freshen up a bit." She kept the washcloth at her throat as their gazes met again in the mirror. "You made quick work of the boxes."

"I brought up a couple that look promising. Some interesting photographs to sort through. I'll go down and get the rest later."

She nodded as she leaned against the sink for balance. Hard to believe she'd initially had reservations about letting him go through her dad's things. Now she was eager to join him in the hunt. Her change of heart was a prime example of how quickly her feelings for him had evolved. Maybe too quickly. From disgraced cop to trusted partner in just two short days.

If she'd given him any thought at all in the years since he'd left the department, it had been the passing worry that she might find herself on a similar path. That she might reach the peak of her profession only to flame out in her thirties as he had. The attributes that drove her to compete and succeed were also the flaws that could end her career as a detective.

She wasn't proud of the fact that she'd passed judgment on him without bothering to dig into the specifics of his downfall. His appeal had caught her off guard because she'd primed herself to dislike him. His attractiveness only seemed unassuming at first, but then his magnetism had a way of hitting like a ton of bricks. How had she never noticed back in the day how truly beautiful his gray eyes were? Or the sensuous shape of his lips and the strong line of his jaw? The hint—just a hint—of swagger in the way he carried himself?

His hair was tousled as if he'd been driving with the windows down, and his shirt was untucked and unbuttoned, revealing another worn T-shirt beneath. What she'd once considered a careless and lackadaisical approach to his appearance now seemed understated and unaffected. A man who was comfortable in his own skin.

All this flashed through her head in the blink of an eye as he held her gaze in the mirror. Then he came down the hallway slowly, pausing in the doorway as if worried he might be overstepping his bounds. Her bathroom was a private domain, after all. But she didn't utter a word of protest when he moved up behind her and rested his hands briefly on her shoulders.

Reaching around, he gently parted her collar. "What happened to your neck?" His voice was both hushed and sharp. His gaze probed her reflection. "How did you get those marks?"

"It's not what you think. Not entirely what you think," she amended. "I got a little aggressive washing up."

"You call that washing up? It looks like you tried to scrub off your skin." His hands slid back to her shoulders, and he squeezed ever so lightly. "What happened at the station?"

She felt a shiver go through her at his touch. "I hardly know where to start. It was a very strange afternoon."

And getting stranger by the minute, she decided. Trent Gannon in her bathroom making her go weak in the knees every time their gazes met in the mirror.

"Start anywhere," he said. "Just tell me what happened."

He dropped his hands from her arms and reached for her crutches. A part of her wished that he hadn't. The gentle pressure had been reassuring. Cleansing. She sighed again and accepted the crutches. "Let's go into the other room where we can get comfortable. I'll finish up in here and be out in a minute."

He left her alone and closed the door behind him. She finished washing up. When she came down the hallway a few minutes later, he stood at the window with her dad's binoculars looking down on the property next door.

"What's going on?"

He answered without turning. "Just wondering if your neighbor is home. I can't tell from here if his car is in the garage."

"He left earlier right after you did," she told him.

He swung around at that. "*Right* after?"

"A few minutes later. Why?"

"I'm curious about the timing." He lowered the binoculars as she came up beside him. "What did you mean when you said you'd had a wild afternoon? What happened at the station?"

"The lieutenant had me come in so that he could tell me Gabriel Mathison has been arrested for murder."

Trent looked taken aback by the news. "When did that happen? How did it happen?"

"I was surprised, too," she said. "Stunned might be a better word. Apparently, one of his friends contradicted his alibi. Once his lie was exposed, he came clean about his whereabouts on the night in question. He admitted to having an argument with Jessica King in the parking lot of her apartment complex, but he swears she was alive when he left her."

"That's a pretty big admission."

"Though not a confession," she pointed out. "But get this. Right after the friend came forward, an anonymous caller placed him in the vicinity of where her body was discovered. The police were able to get a search warrant and found blood and hair on a tire iron in the trunk of his car."

"The victim's DNA?"

"We won't know for certain until the lab report comes back."

"That could take a few days." His posture seemed relaxed, but his expression turned pensive. "You said an anonymous caller placed him in the vicinity?"

"Yes, and the caller used a burner phone. The lieutenant thinks it was probably someone who doesn't want to get involved with the police—or the Mathisons—but it just seems a little convenient. I worked on that case for weeks only to have witnesses recant or move out of town. It was like banging my head against a stone wall. Now all this damning evidence turns up out of the blue once I'm off the case."

Trent gave a vague nod as he rubbed a hand across his chin, still deep in thought. "What did Gabriel say about the blood on the tire iron?"

"Naturally, he claims he's being set up. By me, incidentally."

"Of course, he does." His tone was gratifyingly dismissive.

"My history with the Mathisons makes me an easy target," she said. "Who has a better motive to frame him than a suspended cop looking to clear her name? I never thought I would say this, but he may have a point. The evidence could have been planted by someone intent on making him a scapegoat. Maybe the person who murdered Jessica or someone looking to take advantage of an opportunity. Someone with a grudge, maybe. I don't know. All I do know at this point is that the timing worries me. And, yes, I'm well aware of how improbable that sounds coming from me. Two days ago, I literally staked my career on Gabriel Mathison's guilt. Now..." She frowned as she stared down into the backyard. "I want to believe the police have the right man, but something seems fishy about the arrest. I don't trust either of the witnesses or the evidence. I'm not even sure I trust Lieutenant Bertram."

Trent's brows soared. "That's quite a turnaround."

"I'm having to eat a lot of crow lately. It's an acquired taste," she said.

He flashed a grin. "Mathison's arrest was the only reason you were called in?"

"As far as I could tell, but I managed to ask about the cold cases during the course of the meeting. Don't worry—" she was quick to assure him "—I didn't mention anything about the boat or the bloodstained scarf or any other specifics, because I promised you I wouldn't. But I also didn't want to pass up an opportunity. Dan Bertram worked with my dad for years. They were partners for a good amount of that time. I thought he might remember something that could prove helpful."

"Did he?"

She sighed. "Not really. He says he never put much stock in the single-killer theory. It was apparently such a point of contention that he and my dad had a falling out over it. He claimed Dad became so obsessed with those cases that he lost all perspective. Finding the killer was like a personal vendetta for him."

"Your dad was a homicide detective. Of course it was personal. He became the voice of the victims," Trent said. "It doesn't get more personal than that."

She gave him a grateful nod. "The lieutenant insisted that the whole missing shoe thing started when the first victim's fancy high heel was found in a parking garage and the press ran with an abducted Cinderella story."

"Sounds like he went out of his way to try and discredit your dad's entire investigation. Were you aware of any bad blood between them?"

The question surprised her. "Not really. I mean, they had their disagreements. They could both be stubborn and strong-willed. But even after they were no longer partners, the lieutenant would come over for dinner at least once a month. He was there for my dad when my mom walked out, and he was there for me when Dad passed away. He's the one person I thought I could always count on. But today..."

Trent's tone gentled. "Today?"

"Something was different. I can't really put my finger on it, but he seemed distant. Secretive. Maybe he's starting to resent all the trouble I've caused him. Or maybe he was just tense about the arrest. He had to know Richard Mathison would raise hell when he found out. And, boy, did he ever."

"You saw him?"

She grimaced. "I couldn't avoid him. He stormed into the office while I was there. The odd thing is, he was so focused on tearing the lieutenant a new one that he didn't seem to notice me at first. At least that's what I thought. When he finally turned to acknowledge my presence, I had a feeling he'd known all along I was there."

"What did he say when he saw you?"

Her hand crept back to her throat. "He came at me so quickly I was caught off guard."

Trent's gaze narrowed as his voice hardened. "What do you mean, he *came* at you?"

"I thought he was going to attack me. I tried to jump out of the way and lost my balance. He grabbed my shoulders and made it look as if he tried to keep me from falling. But I saw a look in his eyes, and he actually licked his lips when he put his hands around my throat—"

"He did what?"

Trent's outrage caused Sydney to jump.

"Sorry," he muttered.

She laughed nervously. "Not your fault. I'm still a little jittery, I guess. He didn't hurt me, and the whole thing was over in a flash. No one else even saw what he did. Somehow, that made his actions even creepier. That he could be so blatant and sneaky at the same time. But in hindsight, a part of me wonders if I overreacted. Maybe I saw him as a monster because that's how I've begun to think of him."

"Maybe you've begun to think of him as a monster because he is one." Trent's eyes glinted dangerously. "You were right when you said these are not good people. Maybe Gabriel's violent history is learned behavior."

"Like father, like son?"

"Nurture over nature. It's a cycle," Trent said. "What I want to know is, where was Dan Bertram this whole time? Why did he let Mathison get that close to you?"

"He was behind his desk and couldn't see what was actually happening. And I think he may have been as startled as I was at first. Mathison obviously wasn't trying to hurt me. His fingers were around my throat for only a split second, and he didn't apply pressure. It was almost as if he caressed me. Between that and the lip-licking—" she gave an exaggerated shudder "—I think I would have preferred he strangle me. It was like waking up in the hospital to find Gabriel staring down at me. Nightmarish and creepy. Maybe you're right about a cycle. There is something seriously wrong in that family."

"Maybe we need to do a deeper dive into Richard's background," Trent suggested. "What do we even know about him except that he's a rich entrepreneur with enough shady ties and ready cash to get himself installed as a city council member? Not a bad position to have if one needs to keep tabs on current police activities. Or hide sleazy business dealings."

Sydney nodded. "I did some research when I first started investigating Gabriel. Richard and his first wife split years ago when Gabriel was still a kid. Richard sued for full custody and won. I don't think his ex could compete with his high-powered attorneys."

"Is she still in the picture?"

"Not that I'm aware. If she is, she keeps a low profile."

"Where is Richard Mathison now?"

"At this minute, you mean?" Sydney shrugged. "I have no idea. I left the station almost immediately. I didn't see him again."

"And Gabriel?"

"He's in custody until bail is set. The hearing could take up to forty-eight hours."

Trent turned to stare down at her, his expression troubled. "I feel like this is my fault."

She shivered at the intensity of his gaze. "Your fault? How do you figure that?"

"I should never have come to see you in the hospital, let alone at your apartment. I feel like I brought all this to your doorstep. It was never my intent to put you in danger. I hope you know that."

"Of course I know that," she said almost fiercely. "Richard Mathison was gunning for me long before you came into the picture. You didn't bring anything to my doorstep. I knew the risks when I went after Gabriel, but I did it anyway. I don't always do the safe thing or even the smart thing. I do what feels right at the time. If that gets me into trouble, so be it."

He allowed a brief smile. "Maybe we're too much alike to be partners."

"Just a few short days ago, I would have taken exception to that comparison," she admitted.

"And I wouldn't have blamed you." His hand came up once more to smooth back her hair.

"Trent?"

"Yeah."

"I'm going to say something that might make us both a little uncomfortable. Which is surprising. I'm not usually so bold. But I feel like in our case we'd both rather have everything out in the open."

"Speak your mind."

She drew another long breath and released it. "Is it my imagination or is something happening here? Between us, I mean."

His response was instant. "It's not your imagination."

She didn't know whether to be relieved or agitated. "The lieutenant warned me about you."

"What did he say?"

"That you're damaged goods."

His voice lowered to an intimate murmur. "He's not wrong. Maybe you should listen to him."

"You're not damaged. You're wounded. There's a difference."

"Is there?"

"Yes," she insisted.

Something flickered in his eyes. Doubt? Regret? Unease? She suddenly had second thoughts about her own honesty.

"Now I really have made you uncomfortable."

"I'm not uncomfortable. Surprised, is all. Maybe even a little humble. That's a new one for me," he added with irony. "At the risk of sounding like a jerk, I think we should just relax and take our time. See what happens. You've had a shock. Your judgment might be a little off-kilter. Now is probably a good time to remind yourself that you've known me for all of two minutes."

"Two long minutes. Look at all that's happened since you came to my hospital room. That seems like a lifetime ago."

"That's my point. You've been through one traumatic event after another. What you're feeling right now may be a reaction to all that stress."

"Are you trying to convince me or yourself?"

He searched her face. "Both, I think. I'm no expert on relationships, but I do know this. Rushing headlong into any situation with little regard to possible consequences is rarely a good idea."

She nodded. "On that we agree. My impulses have a tendency to get me in trouble. And, full disclosure, I've never been that great at relationships of any kind. Any partner that's ever been assigned to me usually ends up hating or resenting me."

"I doubt that's true."

"It is, and you know it. I had a reputation even before you left the department, and it hasn't softened over the years." She paused. "For whatever reason, you and I work well together. I don't want this other thing to screw that up."

"I don't want to screw it up, either."

"So…" She shrugged.

"So we relax, we take things slow, and for now, we get back to work," he said. "Does that sound right to you?"

Yes, of course, it sounded right and logical and smart. And disappointing. "Where do we start?"

He nodded across the room to where he'd stacked boxes on the floor by her dining table. "We have a lot of information to sort through. Your dad's files are the first priority."

A spark of anticipation ignited despite her deflation. "Okay, but you still haven't told me about your afternoon. What was the task that ate up your time?"

"We'll get to that. Are you hungry? Maybe we should order dinner before we get started."

"Let's wait. I don't think I could eat a bite at the moment."

The return to more mundane conversation helped restore her equilibrium. He was right. Taking things slow was the smart thing to do—not just for her but for him. She wasn't such a prize in the romance department. She had trust issues, probably abandonment issues, and over the years, she'd become far too suspicious of any act of kindness. But—and this was hard to ignore—Trent wasn't like any other man she'd ever dated. His outer appearance to the contrary, he was deep, pensive and insightful. He'd known instinctively that her dad's vendetta against the killer stemmed from his resolute commitment to the victims and that meant more to her than she could say.

Her past perception of him as a disgraced cop had been replaced by the reality of a selfless man who'd given up his dreams—essentially his life—to care for his young sister. A man who had hit rock bottom in grief but managed to lift himself up without becoming bitter or jaded. Sydney had an image in her head that only grew stronger the longer they were together—Trent at his sister's bedside, holding her hand, reading to her, administering whatever comfort he could give her. Then Trent alone in his car on the long drive home when hope had been lost and the only thing left was to wait.

That was the Trent Gannon she'd come to know in just two short days. That was the man she would readily trust with her life if it ever came down to it.

Rather than joining him at the table. She moved across the room to the hallway, turning to glance over her shoulder until she had his attention. He was on the phone. He laid it on the table and followed her to the bedroom without a word.

Chapter Ten

He took her crutches and propped them against the wall. Then he lifted his hands to cup her face and kissed her for the first time. Maybe it was the moment, maybe it was the adrenaline, maybe it was Trent himself, but she couldn't remember ever responding to a kiss so intensely.

His hands slid around her waist as his tongue probed deeper. Balancing on one foot, she wrapped her arms around his neck and leaned into him, shivering when he lifted her. It was still daylight outside, but the bedroom was cozy and dim. They fumbled with buttons, snaps and zippers. Laughing at the struggle of tugging pants over her cast. Then crawling between the cool sheets.

Sydney turned on her side, and he draped his arm over her breasts and nudged her neck with his lips.

"Top drawer of the nightstand on your side," she said.

The drawer slid open and closed. "Full box," he said. "Should I be intimidated?"

"Full *unopened* box, so no. I'm not very sociable."

"Is that what the kids are calling it these days?" His arm came back around her.

"At the risk of spoiling the moment, can I just say something?"

"I doubt I could stop you."

Rolling to her back, she gazed up at him. "Earlier when you were waiting for me, I could tell you were worried. That's why you sent those text messages, isn't it? That's why you wanted to be here when I got home."

His expression sobered. "I was worried. Maybe that's something we need to get into before we go any further."

"That's not why I mentioned it," she was quick to explain. "We don't need to talk about at this very minute. I've more to tell you, too, but we've got all night for that. I only brought it up because I wanted to say…thank you."

"For what?" He sounded surprised.

"For giving a damn about what happens to me. It's been a long time since anyone cared enough to worry."

"That can't be true."

"It's only a slight exaggeration," she insisted. "The indifference to my suspension hit hard earlier at the station, but I've only myself to blame. I've never gone out of my way to make friends at work or anywhere else. People think I'm standoffish and competitive, but mostly I'm just wildly insecure."

"That could probably be said for most of us."

The intimate timber of his voice made her shiver. "Anyway…thank you."

He was silent for a moment. "This day has taken more than its share of unexpected turns."

She couldn't help but laugh. "An understatement if I ever heard one. Lying naked in bed with Trent Gannon…who would have ever thought?"

"Second thoughts?"

"Nope. You?"

"Not a one." He leaned down and kissed her until she was breathless, and then he trailed his lips over each breast, teasing with his tongue before gently nipping with his teeth.

He moved lower still, parting her thighs and lingering there, too, until her soft sighs turned into sharp gasps.

Plunging her fingers in his hair, she pulled him up and into her. He obliged, dipping his head to kiss her again. Moving in such a way that had her trembling from head to toe. He was good. Very, very good. The tension became white hot. She lifted her arms and clutched the headboard as her body shuddered in release.

THEY GOT UP at some point and showered. Trent helped her with the plastic cast cover and all the minor tasks that she'd taken for granted before the accident. Afterward they went back to bed and napped. When Sydney woke up, it was dark outside, and she was alone.

Her phone was in the other room. She had no idea what time it was, but she had the sense that it was still early. She dressed and tottered down the hallway to find Trent at the table going through her dad's files. He glanced up when he heard her come in, smiled in that way he had before he beckoned her to join him.

"What time is it?" she asked as she crutched around the sofa.

He glanced at his phone. "Nine thirty-three."

"When did you get up?"

"A little while ago. I wanted to get in a few hours of work before I have to leave." When she lifted a brow, he said, "I need to be home by midnight."

"The boat. Of course," she said with a nod. "Why didn't you wake me up? I'm supposed to help with those files."

"You were sleeping peacefully. I figured you needed the rest, and I felt pretty energized. Thank you for that," he added with a knowing smile.

"If only I could take credit," she countered. "We both

know the real reason for your excitement. You couldn't wait to dig into these files. That's not an accusation, by the way." She moved up behind him and rested a hand on his shoulder as she peered down at the open folder in front of him. "Find anything interesting?"

His hand came up to briefly rest on hers. Then he released her and was all business. Fine by her. They had a lot of work ahead of them, and she was as excited as he was by the prospect of the hunt.

"The files were a bit of a mess," he said. "Did you go through the boxes before they were stored?"

"No. I didn't have time. There was so much that had to be done before I could put the house on the market. Why?"

"Your dad's notes are thorough, but the condition of the files leads me to wonder if he went through the boxes looking for something in a hurry. I found dozens of loose photographs. For whatever reason, he never went back and refiled them. I've done my best to label them." He indicated three separate stacks on the table. "For our purposes, I've grouped them into crime scene photos, victim photos and miscellaneous. The next step is to locate the corresponding casefile and return them to the proper folder."

"Doesn't seem like something Dad would do," she said. "He was always so organized. Everything in its proper place at home and at work. What do you think he could have been looking for?"

Trent shrugged. "Your guess is as good as mine. Maybe we'll figure it out as we go along."

"What's in the miscellaneous stack?" she asked.

"Photos that don't fall into either of the other two categories but, for whatever reason, piqued my curiosity. I figured they must have had some significance to your dad's investigation if he kept them with his notes."

She sat down at the table and leafed through the crime scene photos. An image jolted her as she flipped back through. Pulling the photograph from the stack, she placed it face up so that Trent could see the one that had caught her attention.

His expression turned grim. "The second victim. She stands out from the others because the savagery of the attack appears to be an anomaly. Much more violent and graphic than any of the other murders. I think I've figured out why. The first victim—"

"The missing Cinderella," Sydney interjected.

"Correct. She was executed with a single gunshot to the back of the head. The detectives who investigated the case could never find motive. No enemies, no nefarious connections. For years, they believed her death was either the result of mistaken identity or she'd been caught in the wrong place at the wrong time. Maybe she saw or overheard something that got her killed. The second murder nearly a year later and thirty miles away was an entirely different situation as you can see from that photograph."

Sydney's gaze dropped back to gruesome image. "We call this kind of brutality overkill. Usually the result of rage or revenge. A crime of passion. The first murder appears to have been a cold, premeditated execution. No wonder the cases were never connected. Different jurisdictions, completely different MO."

"If not for your dad's persistence, no one would have ever suspected a single perpetrator. You should be proud of him," Trent said.

"I've always been proud of my dad." She returned the photograph to the proper stack. "If the second victim was the only one subjected to that level of savagery, maybe the killer knew her. Maybe the attack was personal."

"That's one explanation," Trent said. "But I think in those early years he was still evolving. Experimenting. Searching for the perfect method of taking a life that would give him the greatest thrill. Try putting yourself in his head for a moment."

Sydney shivered. "I'd rather not."

"Then let me do it for you." He lowered his voice as his gaze held hers across the table. "Let's assume you've never killed before—"

"For the record, I haven't."

"Let's *assume* you've had a dark urge for as long as you can remember. A need that has only grown stronger with each passing year. You try to assuage the hunger by fantasizing and possibly stalking, but a day comes when those fantasies no longer cut it. The desire to take a life becomes overpowering, all-consuming. You begin the hunt for a victim. Now that the decision has been made, the craving intensifies. But you're smart. You realize the importance of planning and a meticulous attention to detail. Nothing left to chance. You wait for the perfect opportunity in order to minimize exposure and the risk of getting caught. But as careful as you are, it's your first time and you're nervous. Strung out on adrenaline. You've had months if not years to work up the courage, but when the moment is finally at hand, you just need to get it over with before you lose your nerve. Like ripping off a bandage."

Sydney stared at him in silence.

"Death is quick and clean," he continued. "One shot to the back of the head and it's done. But the initial high begins to fade rapidly. You're left frustrated. Unfulfilled. You watch and you wait until you find a second victim. The scrupulous preparations only heighten the anticipation, so you take your time. When the moment finally arrives, you're more excited than nervous. Almost euphoric. The adrenaline is pumping so hard you find yourself losing control, overcompensating for that first sterile kill. Not quick and clean like before, but in the end, still unfulfilling because the rage you've worked yourself into steals the moment. You may even have blacked out at some point. Afterward, you have nothing but a few hazy images to sustain you until the next kill."

Sydney muttered an oath. "You made that seem too real."

"Just getting my point across."

She let out a slow breath. "You've given this a lot of thought."

"Yes." His gaze met hers. "It's become personal for me, too."

"No wonder. He left that scarf at your house. He's been watching you and your neighbors. He's probably been listening to your podcast. I'd take it personally, too, if he sought me out."

"That may have been my motivation at first, but the longer I study these cases, the more I realize how forgotten these victims are. They still need a voice, and if not me, then who? It's like I said before, no one else is out there looking for the killer. It's just you and me."

"Then we need to find him," she said. "For the dead, for their families and before there are any future victims."

He nodded. "And for your dad."

"For my dad." She glanced at the stack of files. "You said you thought the killer was evolving and experimenting in the early years. Why do you think his last three kills were strangulations?"

"Clean but not quick. He could remain in control of his faculties and prolong his victim's death for hours."

"If he *is* active again, things have changed," she said.

"He's older now. It can't be as easy to subdue his victims. Have you considered the possibility of a partner?"

"He's older but not elderly," Trent said. "Probably somewhere in his early fifties to early sixties. Still vital if he's taken care of himself for the past twenty years. But the partner thing is an intriguing idea. That's only one of the reasons I like working with you. You aren't afraid to consider possibilities that on first mention seem remote."

"The lieutenant would probably tell you that's a flaw not a virtue," she said dryly.

"Then he'd be wrong. And speaking of Dan Bertram, I need to show you what I've found." Trent removed a photograph from the miscellaneous stack and handed it to her. "I doubt this has anything to do with your dad's investigation, but for whatever reason, he stuck the picture in one of the boxes. No names on the back, just an address. Does it mean anything to you?"

She stared down at the outdoor shot of a group of thirty-something men standing in front of a corresponding number of adolescent boys. The photograph fascinated Sydney. She said almost in awe, "The man on the far left is Lieutenant Bertram, as I'm sure you've already determined."

"Any idea who the others are?"

She scanned the faces before glancing at the back of the photograph. The scrawled address shook her. "That's the house next door."

Trent nodded. "I thought so."

"I didn't recognize it at first." She flipped the photo back over and focused on the surroundings. "It was taken in the backyard before the pool was put in. The landscaping looks completely different now, and the house has been painted white. I don't know the other men, but—" she tapped the visage of one of the boys "—I think that's Brandon Shaw."

"What?" He took the photograph from her hand. "How did I not notice him before?"

"He was just a kid and looks change over time. A lot of things change. He was called Donnie back then."

He glanced up in surprise. "How do you know that?"

"I had a long conversation with Martin Swann this afternoon."

"The landlord?"

"He caught me sneaking into the garage next door," she said.

Trent gave her a look that seemed to mingle frustration with a hint of amusement. "And here I thought you were going to play it safe unless I'm around to have your back."

"I fully intended to, but the opportunity presented itself and I couldn't resist."

"I guess you'd better tell me the rest," he said with a resigned sigh.

"I was just going to have a quick look around while I waited for my ride, but then Martin came into the garage behind me. Snuck up on me, actually. I'd just opened the freezer lid—"

"Opened *what*?"

"There's a huge chest-style freezer in the garage. Coffin-size, you might say. It struck me as odd that Mrs. Dorman would need that much storage space. And then the possibility occurred to me that I might find her body stuffed inside."

"I guess that's not entirely irrational."

"Martin came in and startled me before I got a good look at the contents. I told him that I'd walked over to ask about Brandon's online class."

"Did he buy it?"

"I'm not sure. He said he needed to get a garden rake that he'd loaned Mrs. Dorman before she left. We got to talking, and with a little coaxing, he told me about Brandon's history. He didn't live next door with his family like he claimed. The place was once a halfway house for adolescent boys being released from juvenile detention. Martin said the kids were each assigned a mentor. Someone known and respected in the community. An authority figure."

"Like a cop," Trent said.

"Or a coach or a businessman, but, yes, like a cop."

"Did Dan Bertram ever say anything about being a mentor?"

"Not to me, but he's pretty private when it comes to his personal life."

"Your dad must have known," Trent said. "How do you suppose the photograph came to be in his possession? And why keep it with his murder file?"

"That's a very good question." Sydney took the photograph from Trent, letting her gaze linger on Brandon Shaw's youthful visage. Even at so tender an age, he'd had those piercing eyes. She took a second, closer look. "That's not possible," she said in a near whisper.

"What isn't?"

"No wonder he looked so familiar when we first met. I couldn't put my finger on why. Hold on. I need to check something." She opened her laptop and searched through her image folders until she found what she needed. "The eyes are a dead giveaway. Why didn't I see it before?"

"See what before?" Trent demanded.

Her voice rose in excitement. "Do you remember when I told you I'd researched Richard Mathison's background? He and his wife divorced when Gabriel was just a kid. Twelve or fourteen, I think. This is a photograph of father and son leaving the courthouse after Richard was awarded sole custody. That trial was pretty sensational for Seaside. The local paper carried all the sordid details for weeks." She enlarged the computer image and turned the screen toward Trent. "Look at Gabriel's eyes. And Richard's, for that matter."

He studied the screen, then picked up the photograph of Brandon Shaw. His gaze darted back and forth between the images before he glanced up. "They could be brothers."

"What if they *are* brothers?"

He repeated the obvious. "Brandon Shaw and Gabriel Mathison?"

"Martin told me that Brandon showed up at his place years after the halfway house was shut down. He claimed he'd found his biological father through a public DNA database. He was a rich businessman who helped Brandon out financially. But according to Martin, the money didn't come without a price. He thought the father had bought Brandon's silence in order to protect his reputation."

"And you think that rich businessman was Richard Mathison." It was a statement not a question.

"It explains why Brandon looked vaguely familiar when I first met him. You saw it, too."

"If you're right, you have to wonder if Richard knew he had another child or was the return of the prodigal son a surprise?"

"I bet he knew," Sydney said. "There were accusations of serial adultery at the trial. Maybe Richard was already married to Gabriel's mother when Brandon's mother got pregnant. Rather than owning up to his responsibilities, he incentivized her to disappear."

"Incentivized her how?"

She shrugged. "Money, threats...probably both. Who knows how Brandon ended up in the system? Maybe his mother died, or for whatever reason, she thought he'd be better off in foster care. I doubt he found Richard through a DNA database. He probably searched for years. He may have even seen a photograph of Gabriel in the paper and put two and two together."

"So he turns up in Seaside to…what? Put the screws to Richard?"

"Makes more sense than returning out of nostalgia," she said. "Instead of giving him money outright, Richard offered him the job of spying on me. Or maybe Richard sought *him* out. He needed someone he could trust to do his dirty work."

"This is nothing more than wild speculation," Trent said.

"I prefer to think of it as brainstorming. Taking all the tiny and obscure puzzle pieces we've collected so far and trying to make sense of them."

"I need to add a piece to the puzzle," he said. "And just to be clear, I haven't deliberately withheld the information. We've had a lot to go through."

Sydney gave him an accusing look. "Shoot."

She listened in fascination as he told her about witnessing trash bags being thrown overboard from the cruiser the night before, the subsequent break-in at his house and the clue that was left on the whiteboard in his office. Then he recounted his solo foray into the woods that afternoon and the cross he'd found in the clearing that corresponded to the icon on the map. When he described the feeling of being watched, she felt a shiver go through her.

"You never saw anyone?"

"No. For a while, I thought I'd imagined the whole experience, but I didn't dream up that cross or the bouquet of wilted roses that someone had place at the base. *White* roses."

"*White* roses?" she repeated with the same emphasis.

He pulled a plastic evidence bag from one of the boxes and handed it to her. "There's a card inside the envelope.

The ink is a little runny from the rain, but the message is still legible."

"What does it say?"

"You should probably take a look for yourself."

She opened the bag and removed the card from the damp envelope. Her heart was already pounding by the time she deciphered the smeared message: *See you soon, Sydney.*

Chapter Eleven

A little while later, Sydney stood at the window peering down into the dark backyard. Trent was still at the table sorting through the boxes. He seemed tireless in his mission.

"What's going on over there?" he asked without glancing up.

"Looks like he's home. There's a light in the sunroom."

"I wonder why we didn't hear his car drive up."

"Maybe he's been home this whole time." She heard a chair scoot back from the table, and a moment later, Trent joined her at the window.

"You can see right into his house when the lights are on," he said.

"Which means he can probably see right into mine. Maybe we should move away from the window." But they both remained in place, as if glued by a morbid curiosity that rendered them immobile.

"I'm still trying to make sense of something." She shifted her body weight to a more accommodating position on the crutches. "The message you found on the card with the roses is identical to the one left in my hospital room. And it's the same catchphrase Brandon Shaw uttered from the bottom of the stairs when I first met him. That's one of the reasons I've been so suspicious of him. I don't think the phrasing or the timing was a coincidence. To take it a step further, if he's the one who lured you into the woods this afternoon, was he also the intruder who left the cross symbol on the map in your office? Is he the person piloting the boat night after night?"

"All very good questions," Trent said.

She gave him a sidelong glance. "Here's an even better one. How did he manage to get his hands on a scarf that belonged to a woman who was murdered twenty years ago? As you pointed out earlier, he would have been a kid back then."

"A troubled kid with a cop for a mentor."

"Meaning?"

He frowned. "I keep going back to that photograph. I have to believe your dad kept it for a reason. And I'm starting to wonder if he and Dan Bertram were as close as you thought they were."

"The lieutenant did say they had a falling out over my dad's single-killer theory. He also said they put any hard feelings behind them when they became partners."

"Maybe they became partners because your dad felt the need to keep a close eye on him."

She shot him a glance. "You're not suggesting what I think you are."

"I'm thinking out loud," he said. "You mentioned earlier that you're starting to have doubts about him."

"About his honesty and his relationship with Richard Mathison. Not about *that*," she insisted. "Being a bent cop is a far cry from being a serial killer."

"Like I said, just thinking out loud."

"Then think about this. Richard Mathison accused me of being smug and self-righteous just like my dad. I had no idea they even knew each other."

"Maybe that explains the photograph," Trent said. "If

your dad noticed the resemblance between Brandon and Gabriel, he could have started digging into Richard Mathison's past."

"But why?"

Trent shrugged. "Maybe we'll find that out somewhere in his notes. Did Martin say what happened to Brandon after he left the halfway house?"

"They lost touch for years, apparently. Then Brandon showed up on his doorstep one day with the news about his biological father."

"And then a few years after that, he turns up again in the house next door."

Sydney's attention was still fixated on the lighted sunroom. "We need to get a sample of his DNA."

She felt Trent's gaze on her. "That would require a break-in. If caught in the act, you'd be fired for sure, and we both might end up in jail."

"Or we could just go through his trash," she suggested.

"Even if we could get our hands on a viable sample, we'd still need Richard Mathison's DNA for comparison. Or Gabriel's. But neither is likely to volunteer a swab."

"What about the bloodstain on the scarf? I don't suppose you've heard back from the lab yet."

"Probably not until the end of the week. Why?"

"I'm working on a theory of my own," Sydney said. "It's a little out there, so keep an open mind."

"My mind is open," he assured her.

"It involves the recent murders. Two homicides that appeared to be drug-related and then Jessica King. All three bodies were dumped close to the Mathison beach house. I figured it was a matter of convenience or hubris on Gabriel's part, but my perception of that case is also evolving."

"You think someone has been setting him up all along?"

"Setting him up or trying very hard to get Richard Mathison's attention." She scowled down into the backyard. "Do you know the reason cats leave gifts of dead rodents on their owner's doorstep? It's not about hunger. It's about instinct. It's about sharing skills with the family."

"Nature versus nurture," he murmured.

"The first two victims were deliberately chosen because of their ties to the drug trade. The killer knew the police would draw the most obvious conclusion, but he wanted Richard to know the truth. That's why he dumped the bodies near the beach house, as if to say, 'See, Dad? I'm just like you. You gave away the wrong son. The superior son. The only son worthy of your legacy.'"

Trent turned to face her. "Brandon is jealous of Gabriel and decides to take him out of the picture by framing him for murder."

"Exactly."

"That's some theory," Trent said. "Mind open, mind blown."

"It is just a theory," Sydney reminded him. "No one will believe any of this without concrete proof."

He glanced at his phone. "Speaking of proof... I need to get home before the boat makes an appearance. Who knows? Tonight could be the night when he finally shows his hand."

"I don't like the sound of that," she said.

"And I don't like leaving you alone with a broken ankle. I'd ask you to come with me, but considering the events of the past two evenings, I think you'll be safer here behind a locked door."

At any other time, Sydney would have insisted on accompanying him, but she was realistic about her current immobility. She didn't want to put his life in danger by slowing him down. "I'll be fine. You're the one I'm worried about." She put a hand on his arm. "I'm serious, Trent. Please, please be careful. We could be entering a dangerous phase of the investigation. We're starting to put the pieces together, but we don't yet have the big picture. We don't know who the killer is or who we can trust. We do know he's getting bolder. Brandon Shaw may have moved next door to spy on me, but you're the one the killer has contacted."

"I'll be careful," he promised.

She said in a hushed voice, "The light just went out in the sunroom."

Trent reached over and turned off the nearest lamp.

"The kitchen light," she whispered.

"Why are you whispering? He can't hear us." But Trent complied, circling the room until all the lights were off and they were in total darkness. He came back over to the window. "Can you see anything?"

"It's pitch-black in the yard with the pool lights off."

A moment later, they heard the rumble of the garage door.

"What time is it?" she whispered.

He checked his phone. "Nearly eleven."

"Does that give him enough time to drive to the marina, launch the boat and get to your house by midnight?"

"If he knows what he's doing."

"What *is* he doing?" she murmured.

"Hold on." Trent headed toward the door.

"Where are you going?"

"Just taking a quick look. I'll be right back."

She followed him out to the landing and watched as he slipped through the hedge. Silencing her phone, she eased around the corner. The overhead light in the garage next door was off, but she could see the dim glow from Brandon's open trunk.

Her first thought was that he might be loading a body. She had a sudden vision of Mrs. Dorman's frosted eyes staring up from the bowels of that giant freezer.

Trent returned a few minutes later. He hurried up the steps, and they pressed against the wall as the car backed down the driveway and into the street. The lights were still off as Brandon Shaw sped away from the house.

"What happened?" she asked anxiously. "Did you see anything?"

"He loaded something into his trunk. I couldn't tell what it was."

"Mrs. Dorman," she whispered. "He got rid of her things. Now he's going to dump her body in the bay."

SYDNEY WAS ALONE in the apartment. She hadn't turned the lights on after Trent left, and now the darkness seemed to close in on her as she settled in the recliner and propped up her foot. Her phone was nearby. Trent had promised to keep her apprised of his movements. Not that she would be able to assist if he ran into trouble while tailing Brandon, but at least she could call 911 if he failed to touch base.

She got out her laptop, intent on listening to some of Trent's older podcasts, but she couldn't concentrate. Her mind kept wandering back to their previous discussion. So many questions lingered. Why had the killer gone dormant twenty years ago, and what connection did he have to Brandon Shaw?

On and on her thoughts churned until a sound caught her attention. The same muted thumping she'd heard the night before. She couldn't seem to pinpoint the direction or source. A tree limb bumping against the side of the apartment? A loose shutter somewhere down the street? Nothing suspicious. Nothing to worry about. Except…the wind had died down after a brief rainstorm that afternoon. The night was still.

Easing out of the recliner, she moved to the door and peered through the peephole, then glanced out the side window. No one was around. No one she could see.

She went back to the other window and stared down into Mrs. Dorman's backyard. The lights were still off, and Brandon's car hadn't returned. An inner voice warned her against acting impulsively, but it was nearing midnight. If her suspicions were right about Brandon Shaw, then he would be headed for the marina with Trent not far behind. She would have plenty of time to scoot down the steps, check out the noise and maybe the freezer in his garage and get back upstairs before he returned.

She hobbled down the hallway to retrieve the penlight she kept in her nightstand. A more powerful beam would have been helpful, but she was limited by what she could carry on crutches. Besides, a brighter light might attract attention.

Maybe it was her imagination, but the thumping seemed louder in the bedroom and, to her mind, more frantic.

She followed the sound into the closet. Still muted, still nothing to worry about. But…

Setting her crutches aside, she lowered herself to her stomach and put her ear to the floorboards. The thumping stopped.

She waited. Nothing. No sound at all except for the thud of her heartbeat.

Scrambling to her feet, she grabbed the crutches and went back down the hallway to the front door. She took another quick glance through the peephole, then exited her apartment.

Going down the outside staircase was a little more nerve-racking in the dark. She slid the crutches down first. Without them she felt vulnerable and exposed. She was already agitated, and the rush of adrenaline made her jittery. But she made it to the bottom without incident and grabbed the crutches, feeling more confident as she slipped them in place.

Her initial intent had been to check the freezer before Brandon returned. But she couldn't get that strange thumping out of her head. Maybe something directly beneath her apartment had caused the noise. Like Mrs. Dorman, Martin Swann had converted his detached garage into a workshop and storage space for his gardening equipment. Sometimes her lights flickered when he used his power tools.

Maneuvering around the corner of the building, she tried the side door. It was unlocked, which struck her as odd. Martin was usually fastidious about securing his tools. She only meant to glimpse inside. But then she heard the thumping. Still so muted as to be her imagination. *It's nothing. Go check out that freezer before it's too late.*

She paused just inside the door to the garage to listen once again. Nothing came to her except the low hum of an appliance. A refrigerator? A window fan?

See? Just your imagination.

Reaching behind her, she closed the door to block the glow of her flashlight. Then she swept the narrow beam around the room. Like Mrs. Dorman's garage, the walls were filled with gardening equipment. The space was smaller than next door and an unpleasant odor permeated from the shadows. The smell made her nose itch and her stomach churn. *Probably fertilizer. There's nothing here, so move on.*

She made another pass with her penlight. At the back

of the workshop, another door opened into what she assumed was a storage room. Again, she told herself to go next door and check the freezer. She hadn't left the safety of her apartment just to wander around in her landlord's garage. But now that she was here…

A padlock on the storage room door had also been left open. That really was odd. Why the need for a second lock when he was usually so diligent about keeping the outside door secured?

Sydney approached carefully. She didn't know what she expected to find inside, but the shelves of chemicals and fertilizers seemed almost anticlimactic. She supposed it made sense that he'd double his efforts to keep poisonous pesticides from curious neighborhood children.

She started to back out of the space when the beam of her penlight sparked off a small metal ring in the ceiling. On closer inspection, the ring appeared to be attached to an attic door. But there wasn't an attic above the garage, just her apartment. The best she could tell, the door was directly below her closet.

Her adrenaline was really pumping now. She had a very bad feeling about that door.

Retracing her steps into the workshop, she searched the walls of equipment until she found the metal garden rake that Martin had taken from the garage next door. She managed to drag it back into the storage room—no easy feat on crutches—and then positioned the penlight on one of the shelves so that she could see the metal ring. Balancing on one foot, she hooked a tine through the ring and pulled.

The folding stairs slid down silently on well-oiled hinges. She grabbed the flashlight and angled the beam up through the opening. Leaving her crutches behind, she used her good foot and the handrails to pull herself up. By this time, she was half convinced she would emerge inside her closet. How a trap door in the floor had gone unnoticed all this time was beyond her, but...

She heaved herself through the opening and sat on the edge as she panned the area with the penlight.

Not her closet after all, but a crawl space that had been constructed between her apartment floor and the ceiling of the garage. She shined the light up and over the walls, where narrow shelves displayed a killer's trophies.

She counted seven shoes, including a blue satin high heel with a rhinestone buckle.

The revelation hit her with the force of a physical blow. Martin Swann was the killer her father had hunted for years. All this time, she'd been living above his lair with no clue of his true nature.

She could almost hear her dad's voice in her ear. *There are no coincidences, Syd.* Then, *Get out of there now!*

She had to get to safety and then call the police—

Thump...thump...thump.

The sound came from directly behind her. She turned in dread, moving the beam slowly over the tight space. From the darkest corner, eyes gleamed back at her.

Chapter Twelve

Sydney was so startled she almost dropped the light. She collected herself and focused the beam back into the space where a young woman lay bound and gagged on the floorboards. Sydney thought she must be dead, but then the eyes blinked. Even with the light in the captive's face, she didn't seem to register Sydney's presence. The woman was either drugged or had been there for a very long time. She was so weak, she could barely lift her hand to knock on the wall. *Thump, thump, thump.* Pause to rest. *Thump, thump, thump.* When she moved, the chain attached to a shackle around her ankle rattled.

Sydney swung her legs up and through the opening, then crawled on all fours back into the narrow space. When the woman finally noticed her, she scooted deeper into the corner. The sounds coming from behind the gag were inhuman, like an animal caught in a trap.

"It's okay," Sydney whispered. "I won't hurt you. I'm here to help you. I'm a police detective."

After a moment of frantic keening, the woman seemed to comprehend and quieted.

Sydney lifted her hand to the gag. "I'm going to remove it, but you can't scream."

She nodded, tears rolling down her cheeks.

Sydney couldn't undo the knot. She ran her hand underneath the cloth and managed to work it loose enough that she could slip the gag from the woman's mouth and down her chin.

Her voice was raspy when she spoke. "Can you get me out of here?"

"Yes, but we have to be careful." Sydney checked her phone. No bars. Whatever had been used to soundproof the space also blocked her cell phone signal. "Do you know how long you've been up here?"

"Since last night, I think. We must have been drugged. When I came to, I was chained to the wall. I don't know what happened to my friend—" Her voice caught. "Do you think she's okay?"

"I don't know," Sydney said.

"We just wanted to have a little fun, you know? Unwind in the pool, have a few drinks. But I should have known something was off. A guy like that doesn't need to pick up women in a bar."

"Did he give you his name?"

"Donnie. Just…Donnie." She drew a gasping breath. "We need to find my friend. Maybe she's still in the house. Maybe they haven't come for her yet."

"They?"

"I remember two male voices," she said. "Do you think I dreamed the other guy?"

"I don't think so. But right this minute, we need to focus on getting you out of here."

"Can you call the police?"

"Yes, but I'll have to go downstairs. I can't get a signal up here." Sydney adjusted her position so that she could check the lock on the shackle.

"Can you unfasten it?" the woman whispered.

Sydney followed the chain to a heavy bolt in the wall. "Not without tools. I need to find something to snap the links."

The woman clutched her arm. "Please don't leave me here."

"I'm coming back. I won't leave without you, I promise." She gently pried the woman's fingers from her arm. "Just stay quiet, okay? I'll be back before you know it."

She scooted backward across the rough boards until the lower part of her body was through the opening and she felt for the steps with her foot. A rustling sound caught her attention a split second before a hand closed around the cast and yanked. She screamed in agony and flailed for the railings as she crashed through the opening and landed on her back at the bottom.

A light came on in the storage room. Martin Swann put one foot on either side of her legs and adjusted his glasses as he peered down at her.

"I've waited a long time for this."

Sydney used her elbows to propel herself backward.

"No use trying to escape. You won't get very far on that ankle."

"I know who you are. *What* you are." She nodded toward the opening in the ceiling. "I saw your trophies up there. I saw her."

"I don't think of them as trophies. They're my memories."

"I think of them as proof," she said. "The kind of hard evidence that will put you away for the rest of your life."

"Maybe, if they were to ever see the light of day. But I'm good at keeping secrets. I know how to fade into the background. I'm the kind of guy no one ever notices. The quiet neighbor who keeps to himself. Your dad was the only one whoever got close to finding out about me. So close, in fact, he forced me into retirement. A part of me had to admire him for that. Too bad a heart attack took him out of the game before he knew what I had in store for you. Although I did warn him once."

Don't let her go outside until we catch the bastard.

She inched backward. "Why surface now? You were home free."

"Let's just say the timing was right. The stars lined up. You were always meant to be my last. The daughter of my old nemesis. A fitting swan song."

Sydney's hand bumped against something on the floor. Her fingers closed around the rake handle. The tool was heavy and bulky. Hard to swing from her position. She'd have to be quick—

A whimper came from the crawl space. A tiny sound that drew Martin's attention for one split second. That was enough. She swung the rake against his legs, then into his groin. When he dropped to his knees, she aimed for his head. Blood gushed from the wounds left by the metal tines.

By the time he toppled to the floor, she was already on her feet. She grabbed one of the crutches, tucked it underneath her arm and limped toward the outside door.

She was running, hobbling, stumbling toward the stairs when Brandon emerged from the hedge next door. Fear froze her for an instant, and then she plunged on, ignoring the searing pain in her ankle and the screams from inside the garage. Ignoring the bloodlust in Brandon Shaw's eyes as he dashed toward her. She beat him to the stairs, scrambling up several steps before she heard him behind her. She kept going. If she could just make it to the top and lock herself inside—

Up another step and then another. Almost there—

He had deliberately slowed his pace, enjoying the moment. Relishing the foreplay.

She was almost to the top when he grabbed her broken ankle and twisted. She screamed in agony and rolled to her back, lashing out with her other foot as she hoisted herself onto the landing. He came at her quickly. She grabbed each banister and lifted her body, kicking him square in the midsection with the cast. He faltered, then stumbled back a few steps before he caught his balance.

She was on her feet in a flash. Without crutches, she had to put her full weight on the wounded ankle. She couldn't let that slow her down. Brandon was already taking the steps two at a time. She barely made it inside before he slammed his shoulder into the door. Twisting the dead bolt, she staggered back as he rammed the door a second time.

Whirling, she limped down the hallway to the bedroom. Ignoring the pain. Ignoring the sound of splintering wood. She went straight for the revolver in her nightstand. *Stay calm. Stay calm. Stay calm.* Hard to keep her cool when a killer was crashing through her front door at that very moment.

She barely had time to steady the weapon before he appeared in the doorway. It was dark in her apartment, but she had no trouble finding her target. "Don't move. Don't you dare take another step."

He laughed. "Or what? You'll shoot me on the spot? Not possible. Open the cylinder and check your ammo."

"I said don't move!" she yelled when he took a step toward her.

"Did you really think I'd leave a loaded weapon in your nightstand?"

Was he bluffing? Her hand started to tremble.

"Never mind. I'll save you the trouble." She heard what

sounded like bullet casings hitting the hardwood floor. "See? I told you. You can't stop what's coming with an empty gun."

"But I can," Trent said from the hallway. "Fifteen rounds aimed straight at your back."

"In that case…" Brandon lifted his hands.

Sydney didn't trust his surrender. He had to be up to something.

Trent must have thought so, too. "The police are on the way," he warned. "I wouldn't make any sudden moves."

"They can hold me for twenty-four hours, and then I'll be out and long gone before you even have time to catch your breath."

"Don't count on it," Trent said.

Brandon was still facing Sydney in the dark. "Did you really think I'd start all this without an endgame? I have resources you can't even begin to imagine. You can spend the next twenty years looking, but you won't find me. You won't even know I'm around, but I'll be watching you." He laughed softly. "See you soon, Sydney."

SYDNEY AWOKE TO the unpleasant familiarity of a hospital room. But no Gabriel Mathison watching her sleep this time. No scent of roses permeating the small space. She wasn't alone, however. She could see Trent's silhouette at the window. She called his name and he turned with a smile.

"Hey."

"Hey." She rubbed her eyes. "How long have I been asleep?"

"A few hours. How do you feel?"

"Groggy. What did they give me anyway?"

"Something strong." He sat down on the edge of her bed.

"You were in a lot of pain. They had to remove the old cast and reset the bone."

She sat up suddenly. "The woman I found. Is she okay? They brought her here, too, didn't they?"

"Physically, she's fine. Mentally...that'll take a while."

"And her friend...?"

"The police are out looking, but I'm afraid they won't find her alive."

"That's my fear, too." Sydney lay back against the pillows. "I heard her underneath the floor last night. I thought I'd either dreamed the sound or it was nothing more than a branch brushing against the wall or a loose shutter or..." She trailed off. "I should have investigated. Maybe I would have found both of them alive."

Trent frowned. "Don't do that. Don't fall into the what-if trap. You saved a life tonight. Probably two, if you count Mrs. Dorman."

She said on a gasp, "You found her?"

"She's in Florida with her sister. But they were never going to let that old woman back into her house. As you pointed out, Brandon was already getting rid of her stuff. You saved lives tonight, and you closed nearly a dozen unsolved homicides. Your dad would be proud."

"I wish he could have known justice was coming."

"He knew."

"Martin told me that Dad was getting close. That's the reason he went to ground. I was supposed to be his swan song."

"I've been thinking about that photograph in light of what's happened," Trent said. "Brandon—Donnie—must have found out about Martin. That's how he came to be in possession of the bloodstained scarf. Maybe he squirreled away pieces of evidence as insurance if Martin ever turned on him."

"Or for blackmail."

"That too. I wonder if Brandon said something to Dan Bertram when he was a mentor at the halfway house. Just a throwaway boast that meant nothing to Bertram, but it put both Brandon and Martin Swann on your dad's radar."

"My ending up in that apartment was no coincidence," Sydney said with a shudder. "Martin has been watching me all these years, and I never suspected a thing. Stranger still that he's at this very moment in the same hospital getting the finest medical treatment taxpayer money can buy. Doesn't seem fair. Doesn't really seem like justice."

"You nearly took his eye out with the rake, so there's that. I have a feeling the real justice will be swift when it finally comes," Trent said grimly. "Serial killers don't tend to fare well in Texas prisons."

"And Brandon Shaw? Do you think Richard Mathison will help him disappear? Will I need to watch my back for the rest of my life?"

"Richard may not be willing to help once he finds out Brandon tried to frame his other son. But if it makes you feel any safer, I'll be watching your back, too." He squeezed her hand. "You have more people watching out for you than you know. Bertram came by earlier to check on you. I don't know if he's crooked. My gut says he has a few skeletons. But either way, he seems to genuinely care about you."

"Thanks for that."

Trent stared down at her for a moment.

"What?" she demanded.

"You should know your mother was here earlier, too. Evidently, Bertram called her."

Sydney opened her mouth in astonishment. Then she turned her head to glance at the door. "Where is she?"

"She said she'd be back in the morning. There's been a steady stream of officers coming by to check on you, including the chief. I wouldn't be surprised if you're reinstated without a hearing. You may even get a promotion."

"I didn't do any of this alone," she said. "I would have been blindsided by Martin Swann if you hadn't brought these cases to my attention. You can probably have your old job back, too, if you want it."

He shrugged. "I loved being a cop and I was good at it. But that's in the past. These days, I'm more into looking toward the future."

She gazed up at him. "Can I ask you something?"

"Go for it."

"Is this real? You and me, I mean. Did we ruin things by moving too fast?"

"Time will tell. All I can say for certain is that nothing has felt this right in my life in a very long time."

She nodded. "I feel the same."

He bent and kissed her. "You should get some rest. It's been a long night."

"Will you be here when I wake up?"

"I'm not going anywhere."

She sighed deeply and closed her eyes.

* * * * *

HARLEQUIN
Reader Service

Enjoyed your book?

Try the perfect subscription for Romance readers and get more great books like this delivered right to your door.

See why over 10+ million readers have tried Harlequin Reader Service.

Start with a Free Welcome Collection with free books and a gift—valued over $20.

Choose any series in print or ebook. See website for details and order today:

TryReaderService.com/subscriptions

RSBPA24R

we founded

llaneous stack a

led it to her.